CAPE MAY STARS

CLAUDIA VANCE

CHAPTER ONE

Margaret stood gazing starry eyed towards the street. Right out in front of The Seahorse Inn, and lined up around the block, many film production trucks were parked in coned-off areas. *Dinner under the Stars,* a big-budget movie, was shooting in Cape May for the next two months, and the residents and businesses were abuzz with excitement.

It was early February, and Katherine Duffield, one of the big celebrities starring in the movie, was due to arrive at The Seahorse Inn in a couple of days. She had rented out the entire B&B for the duration of the filming, which made Margaret and Liz both incredibly excited and nervous at the same time. They needed to make sure everything was spotless and up to a celebrity's standards, after all. They had never met a movie star before, let alone had one stay at their B&B.

A crowd of locals gathered outside on the sidewalk taking photos of the film trucks, while cars drove by, slowing to take a look. It seemed everyone in Cape May was talking about the movie, as big-budget productions didn't come around often.

Margaret glanced next door to see John and Rose sitting on their porch watching the spectacle on the street. They looked over at Margaret, smiling and nodding.

"Morning, Margaret. Are you guys ready for all of this? You'll have to fill us in on what Katherine Duffield is like. Boy, they sure took up all the street parking for blocks. I bet some neighbors are *not* happy about that," John said with a chuckle.

Margaret laughed good-naturedly. "It's only for two months, I'm sure those neighbors will get over it. We're actually not quite ready yet. We still have a lot to do."

Rose peeked her head around Bob. "Well, I'll be keeping my eye out for that Katherine Duffield. I'm a huge fan. I've loved her for many years."

Liz stepped out onto the porch with two mugs of coffee and handed one to Margaret. "I heard from the neighbors that these trucks were all parked during the wee hours; apparently, there was a lot of noise around 3 a.m. when they arrived. They sure have taken over the neighborhood already. It's so exciting. I feel like I'm living in NYC again. There were always films shooting around the city when I lived there. I saw celebrities all the time but never got to really meet one. This should be interesting."

Margaret gratefully accepted the coffee and took a deep breath and a sip. "I spoke to Katie, one of Katherine Duffield's assistants, while you were upstairs cleaning. Let's just say, we have our work cut out for us."

Liz wrinkled her brow. "What do you mean?"

Margaret laughed. "Katherine has a full list of demands that we have to abide by. She will pay for it all, but we have to provide it. Wait until you see it."

Liz rolled her eyes. "I'm confused. I thought celebrity riders were only for on-set or at the venue?"

Margaret sat down in a rocking chair, set her coffee down on a small table, and pulled out her phone. "Apparently not. Here's the list they e-mailed me of what we need to do and get for Katherine."

Liz grabbed Margaret's phone and quickly looked the e-mail over. "Bowls of only brown M&M's in every room? White roses with stems cut at exactly 7 inches in vases in every room that need to be replaced every other day? A case of Lauquen Artes Mineral Water in every bedroom? Black Egyptian cotton towels in every bathroom? Are they serious? And we have to provide all of this?"

Margaret sighed. "Yeah. They're paying for it and paying us to get it. Though, I thought we were just providing a place for her to stay. Of course, we could say no, but I feel like she might find somewhere else to stay. I'm just so excited to have her here, I don't mind too much. It kind of makes me feel like we're part of the production team. There's a lot more on that list, though."

Liz sighed and handed the phone back to Margaret. "I'll read the rest later. I'm going to go finish cleaning for now."

* * *

Irene checked into her hotel room in Cape May a few hours after her plane landed in Philadelphia from Los Angeles. The movie would start shooting in a couple of days, and the crew, both local and from afar, were just starting to arrive. Her room was paid for by production, otherwise she would have just stayed with her parents or brother, Dave, as she wouldn't have been able to afford it with her meager earnings.

Irene was a production assistant—the lowest position on set—and it only paid twelve dollars an hour, with overtime after ten hours. Shoot days were usually long, ranging from twelve to sixteen hours, sometimes upwards of twenty. A lot of crew members started out as PAs and worked their way up. The job required her to do anything and everything. Most of the time, she was a First Team PA, which meant she was in charge of keeping track of the actors and escorting them to set, among other things. It wasn't an easy job by any means, and became quite stressful at times when the cast didn't cooperate. She was also much older than the other production assistants, as it was normally a job that college graduates started at.

Irene was almost forty years old, and had left behind an elementary school teaching position she'd held for fifteen years in New Jersey when a bad breakup made her reevaluate her life. During her summer break, she went to visit a friend who was an assistant director on movies in Los Angeles, and that friend asked her if she'd like to be an additional production assistant on a feature film while she was visiting for the month. Irene accepted and ended up falling in love with the excitement of being part of a film crew. Fourteen-hour shoot days were followed by hang outs with the crew at different local restaurants where they'd all laugh and talk for hours, even though they were exhausted and had to be up early for the next day's call time. The crew became like one big family, and being around the cast was especially exciting. She got to travel to different states and countries for work, and her once small town, routine life was now crazy and exciting. Though she sometimes missed her old life—especially when she was on her sixteenth hour on set and exhausted.

The goal for Irene was to someday become an assistant director since a production assistant's salary would never be enough to live off of comfortably. She would have to get all of her PA hours in before she could get into the Director's Guild of America.

After settling in to her hotel room, Irene called Margaret.

"Hey, Irene," Margaret answered.

"Hi, Margaret. I just arrived and am at my hotel, but I wanted to check in to make sure you and Liz are doing OK with the arrival of Katherine. I hear she's a handful. I've never met her, but I will be in charge of her on set."

Margaret smiled. "We're doing OK, but we do have a long list of things we need to get for her here at the B&B."

Irene rolled her eyes. "Figures. They can be so needy, these

4

celebrities. I hear that she has to have her personal chef with her at all times and has many personal assistants."

"I haven't heard anything about a personal chef yet. I thought we'd be the ones providing the breakfasts," Margaret said confused.

Irene laughed. "Oh, I'm sure it will come up soon. I'm surprised they didn't mention it yet. She is known for being very picky about food. It has to be top-of-the-line. I kind of feel bad I dragged you into this by recommending your B&B, actually. Please let me know of anything I can do to help."

"I'm sure it will be fine. How bad can she possibly be? I mean, it's *the* Katherine Duffield. One of the greatest actresses of our time," Margaret said optimistically.

Irene shrugged. "Well, let's hope. I'll feel awful if she ends up taking advantage of you and Liz. Trust me, I've seen my fair share of nightmare celebrities. They seem all nice and wonderful on-screen, but off-screen they are the most self-absorbed, shallow people you'll ever meet. Granted, a lot of them aren't like that."

* * *

Around lunchtime, some of the crew arrived and began opening up the trucks to unload equipment. Liz didn't have a clue where they were actually going to be filming. There was talk of a set being built at a warehouse down the street.

"Hi, Liz. How are you and Margaret making out?" Betty hollered over from her porch next door.

Liz smiled. "We're doing OK. Just have a lot of shopping to do. You?"

Instead of answering, Betty walked down her porch steps and over to Liz with a big giddy smile on her face. "Well, William Hansen has booked the entire Morning Dew Cottage while he's filming here in Cape May."

Liz shrieked, "You're kidding! William Hansen is staying at your B&B? He is a dreamboat."

Betty laughed. "Oh, trust me, I know! How funny is it that we both have big celebrities staying at our B&Bs? And right next door to each other!"

Liz grabbed Betty's hands and squealed like a little girl. "This is so exciting. I can't stand it."

When Liz's cell phone rang, Betty said goodbye and walked back.

"Hey, Sarah. What's up?

Sarah tried to get words out between all of the loud bangs behind her in the background. "Hey, Liz. They're in the home-stretch with construction on the coffeehouse. They were three hours late today, but it's almost finished."

"Oh, that's wonderful! I'm so glad. How are you feeling about it all?" Liz asked.

Sarah paused for a moment. "Well, it is a little scary and nerve-racking, but at the same time exhilarating. I can't believe I'm going through with it. The stars aligned and it all came together so quickly. I'm opening up a coffeehouse!"

Liz smiled and sighed while watching the film crew unload camera equipment from the truck. "I'm so proud of you for following your dreams. You were so lucky to get that awesome location and building. The remodel is going to be gorgeous."

Sarah sighed. "I know. I'm so excited. It's amazing that the bank was in such good condition all of these years. I was delighted to discover that someone had previously started reno-vating, but stopped due to loss of funding. It has made this remodel not as big or long of a job as I thought it would be. Are you sure you and Margaret are going to be OK without me working at the B&B? I know it's bad timing with Katherine Duffield arriving any day now."

"It's perfectly fine. We have Dolly and Kim here, and they're more than happy to put in more hours with all of the excitement going on. Don't worry about us. Focus on your coffeehouse."

After Sarah was laid off from her school guidance counselor position due to cutbacks, she worked part-time helping Margaret and Liz at The Seahorse Inn while researching how to open the coffeehouse she'd always wanted. The excitement of starting a new business must have rubbed off on her. There were a few places to get coffee in Cape May, but none like the one she had in mind.

Sarah had been obsessed with reading books since she was a child, and dreamed of the coziest place to sip hot or cold drinks and curl up with books. This wasn't going to be just any coffeehouse, though. It was also going to have a selection of books for sale, and it was going to have a pet-friendly sitting section, just like her favorite places to get coffee in the city. She loved seeing dogs laying at their owners' feet while they sat in the city cafes drinking lattes and reading or working on their laptops.

She had many aspirations for her business—a projector to show movies, comfy couches and chairs, some turntables with vinyl records, and the best pastries and snacks in town. She'd set her eye on a 112-year-old abandoned bank in Cape May as the perfect place for the coffeehouse. It had unbelievably high ceilings, standing fifty feet high, tall arched windows, and the ornate stonework was breathtaking. Stepping inside felt like stepping back in history; it was perfection. The bank, though still structurally in good condition, definitely needed a remodel in order to be a coffeehouse, which was a pricey endeavor to get the building back in working order and up to code. Thankfully, she'd found a silent business partner who had interest in saving the property to help front the money.

Liz walked back inside as Margaret made her way outside with her keys in hand. "Are you ready to go shopping? We'd better go now before the evening rush hour. Though, I feel like this is going to take hours. We have to go somewhere that sells towels, roses, and food, among others," Margaret said.

Liz rolled her eyes and followed Margaret to her car. "OK, but give me the list. I don't have all night to shop. We're getting this stuff and getting out."

Margaret handed Liz the list, and her mouth dropped. "I know I only glanced at this the first time, but did I really miss all of this? She wants pink rose petals in the toilets? A framed photo of Princess Diana on the dresser? Ten jars of blue cheese stuffed olives? Twenty yoga mats?"

Margaret smiled and sighed. "It's nuts right? But I'm too excited to care. I mean, we're getting asked to shop for *Katherine Duffield*. That's thrilling in itself."

Liz threw the list in the back seat and crossed her arms. "This is madness. These celebrities take it too far. Who does she think she is? The Queen?"

Margaret put the car into drive and slowly made her way out of the driveway, being careful not to hit any of the crew members around the truck parked out front. "Well, let's just get this over with and we can head home for a good night's rest without the worry of having to do it tomorrow."

* * *

After a few hours of shopping, just as they pulled back into the inn's driveway, Margaret received a call from their mother, Judy.

"Hi, Mom. You're on speaker. Liz is with me."

"Hi, Margaret. Hi, Liz," Judy yelled into her phone as if unaware that there was no need to shout in order for the speaker phone to work.

"Hi, Mom. What's up? Why do you have loud Italian opera blasting in the background? Is that your thing now?" Liz asked.

Judy laughed. "Well, that's precisely why I'm calling."

Margaret and Liz looked at each other, confused.

"Your father and I have decided to spend a couple of months abroad. We're starting in Italy and seeing where the wind takes us from there. We got a good deal on one-way tickets today. We leave tomorrow."

Margaret rubbed the back of her neck and twisted the necklace that she wore. "Tomorrow? Are you sure that's a good idea? You've never been abroad before, and Dad barely ever leaves the house anymore with his arm issues. Do you even know Italian? You will probably need to know some depending on where you go?"

Liz sighed. "Mom, we don't think this is a good idea, OK? We're worried about you two."

Judy laughed with annoyance behind her voice. "Well, we're two adults who can make their own decisions. I'm seventy-two and have never done many of the things that I want to do, like go abroad. The clock is only ticking. I want to go live my dreams like you two get to do. Your dad is excited to go too. In fact, Ruth and Bill are coming as well."

Margaret chuckled. "Ruth and Bill? Your friends who get in five car accidents a year because they don't look before they pull out onto roads? Well gee, now I feel better."

Judy let out an exasperated sigh. "Yes, Ruth and Bill. And they only got into two accidents last year, and that was because the other drivers weren't paying attention."

Liz opened her car door. "Well, Mom, thanks for the notice. Please, please please be careful and call or text us so we know you're OK. We just went shopping for Katherine Duffield and now need to unload the car."

"Oh, *Katherine Duffield*. Such an amazing actress. A part of me wants to stay just so I can meet her, but Italy calls my name. You tell her I said hi, OK?" Judy said in a serious tone.

Margaret blurted out a loud laugh. "Yeah, OK, Mom. We'll do that. I'm sure she'll be *thrilled*. Give us a call later. I want to make sure you're all set for this impromptu trip. We worry about you and Dad. You've now given me anxiety on top of the anxiety I already have over hosting a celebrity."

Margaret's heart raced and her palms sweated. Why did she feel like the parent-child roles had been reversed lately with her parents? She worried about them a lot more these days, especially after her father tripped on a potted plant and hurt his arm badly a month ago. Now they were going to be off gallivanting in a foreign country? She took a deep breath and released it slowly while closing her eyes.

Liz poked her head in the front seat. "Are you helping me or what? I thought we wanted to get this over with?"

Margaret popped her eyes open. "Right. Just had to get my bearings after that unexpected call."

Liz eye's softened. "They're going to be OK. Don't worry about it too much. This is what they want to do, and we can't stop them."

CHAPTER TWO

The next morning, Katherine Duffield's assistant called at 6 a.m. while Margaret was still in bed.

"Hello?" she answered groggily.

"Hi, Margaret?"

"Yes, this is she."

"This is Katie, Katherine's assistant. I'm just letting you know that we will be arriving today instead of tomorrow, if that's OK. Katherine insists on coming a day early. We should be there by two, as we're flying in from California."

Margaret, still barely awake, took a moment to compute what Katie said. "Wait. Did you say she's coming today?"

Katie paused. "Yes. Is that OK?"

Margaret, now more awake, sat up in bed and pulled the warm blankets off of her while slipping her feet into the slippers that lay by the bed. "Yes, that's fine. We'll just speed things up a bit for her arrival."

Katie sounded relieved. "Great! Well, we'll see you around 2 p.m. then. Take care."

Margaret stood in her pajamas, staring into the mirror that sat on her dresser. She eyed the new wrinkles on her face and the extra gray hairs that poked out from the front of her head that she hadn't noticed before. She glanced at the clock before walking downstairs to make coffee. This day definitely called for some caffeine.

A couple of hours later, Margaret and Liz headed back to the B&B together. As they pulled into the driveway, men and women with professional cameras were standing around in front of the Seahorse.

Margaret threw the car into park and looked over at Liz. "Is this the paparazzi? How have they gotten wind of Katherine Duffield staying here?"

Liz shrugged her shoulders. "Beats me. Oh, look. Is that Dave talking to one of them?"

Margaret turned to look over her shoulder. Sure enough, Dave was chatting it up with the paparazzi. Someone handed him a business card, and he walked towards Margaret and Liz, who still sat in the car.

Dave leaned his strong arms above Margaret's driver side window. "Hey, you two. Irene called me this morning and told me about this spectacle. I figured I'd get here beforehand to disperse them, but that ain't happening. Some of them have been camped out since late last night. I don't know where they get their information, but they know Katherine is arriving today."

Margaret smiled. "Well, that was nice of you to at least try. Why did someone hand you their business card, though?"

Dave held the business card up and chuckled. "He has a side business of doing family portraits. I'm asking him to leave, and he's pushing his photography business on me. Unreal."

Margaret laughed.

Liz pointed to Hugh and Betty's B&B next door. "There's paparazzi waiting out front of the Morning Dew Cottage too. This place is going to be a circus for the next two months."

Margaret sighed. "Well, the upside is maybe we'll get some good press for The Seahorse Inn. Let's get to work inside. We've got a lot do before she arrives."

Dave opened Margaret's car door for her and gave her a hug and a peck on the cheek. "I can stay and help, if that's alright? Irene wants to stop over later too. I love having my sister back in town."

"Perfect! You can start with picking out only the brown M&M's from these thirty bags we bought," Margaret said with an eye roll and a chuckle.

Dave laughed. "Are you serious?"

"Serious as I'll ever be."

* * *

Sarah stood in the quiet old bank. She took a deep breath and blew it out slowly, admiring the rustic details inside. She was glad they were able to preserve the old craftsmanship. The place had so much character even if it was in disarray still from the remodel finishing up. To think—they were going to demolish this remarkable piece of property by the beach. It bumped up against a row of many other mom-and-pop shops, and had not been in use since 1990.

Since it was raining outside, she set up a spot to work while she waited for the construction crew to arrive for what would be the last few days of work. Fashioning a makeshift desk out of a couple of folding chairs, she opened her laptop. She had to get ready for the new furniture that was arriving in a couple days, put together the employee schedules and go over finances —the list was never-ending.

She heard the creaky, wooden front door open, and looked over expecting to see the construction crew, who were already twenty minutes late. Instead, it was Mark. Sarah smiled and got up to greet him.

Mark shook out his wet umbrella after placing a tall paper bag just inside the doorway. Walking in, he ran his hands through his shoulder-length hair.

"Hey, you. What brings you here?" Sarah asked with a smile as she pulled him into a hug.

Mark hugged her back, then stared up at the tall, cathedral ceiling. He'd been there before, but he still marveled at the wondrous place Sarah had acquired. "Just thought I'd pop in on my way to work. I wanted to see how you were making out. This is a lot for someone to take on themselves."

Sarah's eyes twinkled. "It's stressful, but it's coming along quickly. The construction crew should be here any moment. I imagine the weather might be holding them up."

Mark grabbed the paper bag, which Margaret noticed was from the local bakery, and pulled out two freshly made almond croissants. "I got us these. I have hot cappuccinos in the car as well, but didn't have the extra hands to bring them in. Let me go get them."

Sarah watched him walk back out into the rain, feeling herself swoon over being taken care of. She had never met anyone like Mark. He always paid for everything whenever they went anywhere, he held doors, he showed her affection in public, and he was just all-around dreamy. Being the same age as Margaret, forty-five, she'd only had one serious relationship prior to Mark, but that only lasted two years. The rest of her years, she'd been single. She didn't want to settle down with just anyone, but at the same time had trouble finding "anyone" in the first place. Most men her age were married, but she'd been in the right place at the right time when she'd ran into Mark at that open mic night last year after not seeing each other since college.

Mark walked back in from the pouring rain holding two hot cappuccinos with whipped cream on top. Sarah gratefully accepted the drink and took a sip.

"This is the perfect treat for this rainy day. Thank you."

Mark smiled and made his way to a couple of the folding chairs stacked against the wall. He opened two up, sat on one, and patted the other.

"Come sit with me. I want to enjoy the croissant and cappuccino with you before I get to work."

Sarah threw on her red sweater and tied her brown hair up in a ponytail and a red ribbon bow, and made her way over.

Mark sat silent for a moment. "Not sure if this is a good time to tell you this, but I have to go abroad for work again in a few days. It just came up today. We have a client out in Germany."

Sarah took a deep breath and stared at the floor. "How long will you be gone this time?"

Mark frequently traveled abroad for weeks at a time, and that made it hard for Sarah and him to gain any traction in their relationship. At times, Sarah wasn't sure if she wanted to be with someone who she wouldn't see for long periods.

Mark swallowed hard and put his hand over Sarah's. "It's looking like a month this time."

Sarah felt her heart drop in her chest. She was starting a new business and her boyfriend wouldn't be around during a lot of it. She had strong feelings for Mark, but …

Mark was a forty-six-year-old man who'd prioritized his career over relationships his entire adult life—an eternal bachelor who'd never settled with a woman no matter how drop-dead gorgeous or smart they'd been—but Sarah was different. He was smitten with her, and he had never been beguiled by anyone like he was with her.

Sarah pulled her hand away from Mark, and pushed her stray hair behind her ear while looking in the other direction. "I guess it is what it is. If you have to go, you have to go."

Mark clasped his hands together and looked towards her. "This is not what I want. Trust me. It was exciting twenty years ago, but it gets pretty exhausting these days."

Sarah looked back over at him, then motioned to the grand old bank they sat in. "Well, keep your options open, then."

* * *

15

Katherine arrived with her assistants later that day as expected. A couple of fancy black cars with dark, tinted windows pulled into the driveway one after the other. The driver in the first car got out and opened the back door. Out stepped Katherine Duffield. Her long curly red hair blew in the breeze, and she tilted her oversize round dark sunglasses down and looked the B&B over.

The paparazzi had been ready for the big arrival, and were snapping photos, trying to get that one perfect shot of Katherine Duffield. All that could be heard was hundreds of clicking shutters, firing off in rapid succession.

Margaret and Liz, unsure what to do, decided to stand on the front porch to welcome them inside and answer any questions. Margaret smoothed her floral blouse and looked nervously over at Liz, who didn't seem to be that impressed with the entire situation. Margaret was decidedly more excited about it all than Liz.

Katherine waited by the car with her driver, shielded from the paparazzi with a large black umbrella. Her two assistants walked up to the front porch carrying some of her many pieces of luggage.

Katie stopped in front of Margaret and Liz, holding a clipboard in one hand and large suitcase in the other that she promptly rested on the ground. "You must be Margaret and Liz?" she said, slightly out of breath while extending her hand.

Margaret smiled, nodded, and shook her hand. "Yes, I'm Margaret, and this is my sister Liz. Let us know of anything we can do to make Katherine's stay, and yours, as comfortable as possible."

Katie glanced at Katherine outside talking to the driver, and awkwardly looked back at Margaret and Liz. "Well, there is one thing I forgot to mention. Don't talk to Katherine, and *don't* look her in the eye. If there's a question for her, you can ask one of us."

Liz nearly rolled her eyes and let out a loud laugh she disguised as a cough.

Margaret forced a smile. "OK, we can do that. Whatever she's most comfortable with."

Erin, her other assistant, stopped at the stop of the steps next to Katie, looking completely exhausted. "Hi, I'm Erin. Where can we put all of her luggage?"

"We figured she'd get the nicest room, so that will be the first room on the left upstairs. It's the roomiest and has the best bathroom," Margaret said motioning to the stairwell.

Erin, wiped the sweat off of her forehead with her hand, heaved the overstuffed suitcase off the ground, and made her way inside.

Katie looked at her clipboard and back up at Margaret and Liz. "There were some other things I needed to go over with you guys, but we can get to all that later. For right now, I'll let you know that Katherine is a very picky eater. She brings her personal chef with her whenever she travels for work, so Maria will be arriving tomorrow. She will need to use the kitchen. I'm assuming that's OK."

Liz scrunched her brow. "So, we're not providing any breakfasts or snacks like we usually do here at our B&B?"

Katie looked back at her clipboard. "That's correct. Maria will be providing meals for the assistants and whoever else stays at the B&B with Katherine, as well. It's what Katherine wants. She's particular about smells and what food is around her."

Liz breathed a subtle sigh of relief. "Well, who's in the other cars?"

Katie laughed. "It's all filled with her luggage. Plus, she also likes to have extra cars available for when her friends arrive."

"Friends?" Margaret asked curiously.

Katie looked over at Katherine, who seemed to secretly love the attention from the paparazzi. "Yes, she likes to have them come visit her. It looks like Katherine's coming inside now, so just remember what I told you."

Margaret and Liz stood at attention and tried to look anywhere but at her eyes.

Katherine elegantly made her way to the porch steps in black stilettos, tightly fitted jeans, and a black cashmere sweater, escorted by her driver, who seemed to be enamored with her.

She was tall, about five eleven, and being in her late-forties, had aged gracefully since her twenties. Twenty-five years ago she was featured in her breakout roll, a romance drama based in France, called *C'est la Vie*. She'd starred in many other acclaimed films since, but seemed to be fading from the movie scene over the last ten years.

Katherine walked past Margaret and Liz, only looking at Katie. "I'm assuming everything is ready, and I can go to my room now?"

Katie smiled and opened her arm out towards the door. "Yes, Erin will see you to your room."

"Thank you, Katie."

Katie nervously looked back at Margaret and Liz, trying to hide her embarrassment of how impolite Katherine could be. "Also, one more thing for now. Please don't mention to *anyone* about how she … is."

Margaret nodded, knowing full well what she implied. Liz sighed, feeling over this whole spectacle already.

After Katie walked inside, Liz looked over at Margaret. "What are we supposed to do *exactly*? Just clean the rooms? Are we supposed to be available, but at the same time not be around? I'm confused."

Margaret shrugged. "I guess we'll find out later when Katie gives us more information. For now, let's make the basement *our* area. The home theater is not mentioned on the B&B listing, so I'm claiming it for us as our space."

* * *

18

Irene sifted through the huge stack of call sheets in the honeywagon, which was Hollywood's terminology for a production trailer. Filming would start tomorrow, and the call sheets were the daily shooting schedules that needed to be dispersed. Though it wasn't her job, she had offered to do it anyway. Her job's duties didn't officially start until tomorrow when the actors got there for their first day of shooting. She had done this many times before on past films and knew the drill pretty well. She was feeling overwhelmed with excitement to be working on a big film in her own hometown. Who knew going to LA and starting a new career would bring her full circle, back to where she came from. Still, there was a bit of uneasiness inside of her, and she wasn't sure why.

She hadn't spent any significant time in Cape May, aside from the short visit over Christmas to the B&B with her family, in five years. Not since that terrible breakup, where she'd left her comfy life behind to start anew. She hadn't spoken to Jake, her ex, since that awful day either.

On the upside, Irene had a good feeling about this film. It had a great cast lineup, some of the most talented and respected actors in the business, and the story line was dreamy. It was a romance beach drama set in Cape May, and Katherine Duffield and William Hansen played friends turned lovers, something fans would be thrilled about.

She stepped out of the honeywagon, took a deep breath of salty ocean air, and walked around base camp, getting herself acquainted with where everything was. It was her job to know, after all, since she would be in charge of getting the actors to many of these trailers throughout the shoot. She spotted the actors' trailers, then walked by the hair and makeup and wardrobe trailers. Crew members scurried back and forth, preparing for the first day of the shoot tomorrow. It felt a little like a madhouse. She made her way down the block to a large warehouse behind a restaurant where the set was being built.

Once inside, all she heard was the loud banging of hammers, yelling over the radio, and lumber being thrown about.

She found Brad, one of the set construction workers, sitting on the edge of a platform dangling his legs while taking a break. She scooted up next to him and leaned back on her elbows.

"What do you think about all of this?" Brad said with a smile, happy to see Irene next to him.

The team was currently building the interior set of Katherine's character's house, which was directly next to William's character's house. "I think it looks great. I can't wait to see the final product."

Brad sighed and leaned back on his elbows alongside Irene. "Well, it might not seem like it, but we're running pretty far behind. We had a couple local workers call out the last few days, and it's left us shorthanded. Work on Katherine's character's house is running behind. We're coming down to the wire here, and the producers aren't happy about it."

Irene bit her lip. "Are you still looking for someone to help out with set construction during the shoot?"

Brad jumped up to his feet, and reached his hand out to Irene. "Yep. We're desperate for any kind of help at this point. We've got lots of things to build throughout the shoot."

Irene grabbed his hand, pushed herself up onto her feet, and flicked the sawdust off of her jeans. "Well, I think I may know someone," she said with a smile.

CHAPTER THREE

"Ciao, Liz!" Judy yelled into her cell phone the next day.

"Hi, Mom. I'm assuming you guys made it safely to Italy?"

"Oh, yes! Got here late last night. We checked into our room at the hotel, had a great night's sleep, and ate the most simple but delicious breakfast, a caffe latte with a pastry. We are now off wandering this glorious city of Rome." There was lots of noise behind Judy, making her sound like she was in a crowd.

Liz put her phone on speaker so Margaret, who was standing next to her outside of the B&B, could hear.

"Hi, Mom and Dad. Are you all having fun?" Margaret asked.

Bob, their father, chimed in. "Oh, we are! We're about to head over to the Colosseum. Ruth and Bill want to do a Segway tour, so we might be accompanying them on that afterwards."

Margaret and Liz looked at each other before giggling and shaking their heads. Ruth and Bill seemed much too accident prone to be going on a Segway tour, as well as their own father.

Once Ruth and Bill were out of earshot, Bob cupped his hand over the speaker. "You should see the hats they bought back home for all of us to wear while we're abroad. No way am I putting that *thing* on."

Liz laughed. "What's wrong with it?"

Bob paused. "Bright-red matching cowboy hats with cats eating bowls of spaghetti on them. Think I'm kidding? Think again. I'm trying to blend in here, not stand out for Pete's sake!"

Margaret and Liz laughed uncontrollably picturing their father, who only wore a baseball hat here and there, donning a bright-red cowboy hat, with cats on it to boot. It was comical. Though, he did like cats.

Judy got back on the phone, sounding slightly annoyed with her husband. "Well, now that your father finally got that off of his chest … this city is so fascinating. I can't believe it's taken us this long to visit. Well, we'll talk to you soon. We've got to figure out what direction we need to go in."

"We love you guys. Please be careful and keep an eye on your belongings so nothing gets pickpocketed when you're out in crowds," Margaret said growing concerned again.

Next door at The Morning Dew Cottage, a few fancy black cars with dark, tinted windows pulled into the driveway. The paparazzi, who had been lolling around, waiting for excitement, jumped to their feet, making their camera shutters work overtime from every angle possible.

Out stepped William Hansen. He was tall with a thick head of short gray hair and as handsome as ever. He immediately walked over to some adoring fans who stood on the street. He took a pen out of his navy blue peacoat's interior pocket and began signing autographs and smiling for photographs. Women shrieked at the site of him from down the block, trying to hurry up and get to him before he walked away. He graciously spent a good fifteen minutes meeting his fans.

Margaret and Liz were starstruck, having not taken their eyes off of William yet. They may as well have been the women who shrieked in excitement.

William eventually made his way to the porch, offering to grab his suitcase from the assistant who struggled with the handle, though the assistant declined. He greeted Hugh and Betty as they waited for him on the porch. With a firm handshake and a big hug to each, he made Betty weak in the knees, unbeknownst to Hugh.

Margaret and Liz picked their jaws up off the ground, and finally made their way inside the B&B. William Hansen seemed *nothing* like Katherine. He appeared gracious, friendly, and down-to-earth, where Katherine proved to be just the opposite—a self-absorbed diva.

Dolly and Kim worked the morning and early afternoon hours today, and Margaret and Liz would be relieving them of their duties until after dinnertime.

Dolly and Kim walked out from the kitchen, greeted Margaret and Liz, and grabbed their jackets and personal belongings before making their way out the door to get home.

Moments later, Katie came down the stairs with her clipboard. "So, we have a little issue …."

"What's that?" Liz asked, stuffing her coat in the closet.

Katie glanced out the window at Dolly and Kim getting into their cars, and turned back to Margaret and Liz. "Well, those two ladies you have working here—Dolly and Kim, I think it is? They seem extra excited about Katherine staying here, which is fine and all, but today they knocked on her door and asked for an autograph. That's not really appropriate. Thankfully, Katherine was in the bathroom and only Erin and I noticed."

Margaret placed her hand on her mouth. "Oh no. I will have a talk with them immediately. I assumed they knew not do something like that, but I guess not. I'm so sorry about that. It won't happen again."

Katie nodded. "Yes, that would be great. Otherwise, I'm going to hear it from Katherine, and my job is already stressful enough. Also, have you met Maria yet?"

Liz looked towards the kitchen. "Oddly, we have not. Is she here?"

Katie wrote something down on the paper on the clipboard. "Yes, she is. She has spent most of her time grocery shopping lately, but you'll be seeing more of her soon. She'll be in the kitchen a lot. You may find her a little … interesting. She definitely doesn't like to put herself into a box."

Margaret chuckled. "My kind of lady."

Katie smirked. "Maybe …."

Liz sighed. "Well, we'll be in the basement if any of you need anything. You have our phone numbers too."

* * *

When evening rolled around, Margaret and Liz left the B&B and headed home.

Margaret called Dave.

"Hey, you," Dave said happily into the phone.

"Hey, Dave. How was your day? Want to get a bite to eat tonight?"

"Most definitely. What were you thinking? And my day? Well, it was quite interesting. We can talk about it over dinner." Dave sounding slightly excited.

"Oh! I can't wait to hear. Well, we're driving back to Liz's house now from the B&B, and I'll grab my car and pick you up? I was thinking we could try that new seafood place downtown. What do you think?"

"Sounds great, but what about the girls? Are they with Paul?"

"Yes, they are having an overnight with him tonight. He's been taking them more, which has been great for them to spend more time with their father, especially with everything going on lately. I'll see you shortly."

Thirty minutes later, Margaret pulled up to Dave's driveway at Pinetree Wildlife Refuge. Dave walked out from behind the thick pine trees wearing a red flannel hoodie, jeans, and work boots. Margaret warmed watching him steadily walk to the car. He hopped in, his subtle musky cologne enveloping her, and gave Margaret a hug and a kiss.

"I kind of like being picked up by my lady," joked Dave as he glanced over at Margaret with a big smile.

They got to the seafood restaurant, and the place was alive and busy. Dave put their name in with the host, who immediately sat them at a quiet table for two away from all of the noisy hubbub.

They could see the bustling open-air kitchen from where they sat, and relished being able to see the cooks preparing all of the food. Lavish steaming lobster dinners sat in the window ready to be delivered to the awaiting tables. Their server came by, introduced himself, and took their drink order.

Dave looked the menu up and down quickly before setting it down on the table and casting his gaze solely on Margaret. "I can't wait any longer. I'm bursting at the seams to talk about what happened today."

Margaret looked up from her menu and set it down on top of Dave's. "Well, I hope that means it was a *good* day."

Dave leaned back in his chair, stretching his arms behind his head. "You could say that. Irene found out they need more help with building the sets and other things on the film shoot. She recommended me, they called me today, and I took the job. I'm going to be a part of the set construction team on the film. Can you believe it? The artistic side of me is excited to do something different with my skills."

Margaret plunked her elbows on the table and cupped her face. "Are you serious? That's beyond exhilarating, but how exactly will that work with your job at the refuge?"

"Well, I already talked with them. The refuge is slow in the winter, and they are going to let me work there three days a week instead of five, which gives me extra days to work on the film. By the time the film is done, my regular hours on the refuge will resume."

Margaret smiled, and watched the server set their drinks down on the table. "That's great. I'm really happy for you. How fun will it be to watch this movie when it comes out and see everything you built?"

"What about you? You said something was going on with the girls?" Dave asked, straightening himself upright again.

Margaret rolled her eyes and took a long sip of wine. "Where do I even begin with *that*. Abby and Harper made friends with another pair of sisters at their school over the past few months. Everything seemed great at first, and I was happy they were developing some social lives. Then, things started … happening over the last couple of weeks. I've been so busy with work and the B&B that I haven't had a minute to tell anyone, which is why you're only finding out now."

Dave squinted his eyes. "This is not sounding like it's something good."

Margaret scanned the room, making sure nobody she knew was within earshot. "Well, it started out with their new friends stealing things. I found out they stole the new pens I bought my girls for school, and then they started swiping items from Abby and Harper's lunch boxes while they weren't looking."

Dave shook his head. "Are they poor? Did they maybe not have those things themselves? That seems very odd."

Margaret let out a loud laugh. "Oh, they're far from poor, believe me. I know the parents, but we'll get to *them* later. Anyway, I kind of chalked it up to kids being kids, and didn't think much of it until Abby and Harper came home sobbing last week. These so-called friends of theirs made friends with some other girls. They spread some lies and laughed at and mocked my daughters in front of everyone on the playground. These kids were vicious. You should have heard what Abby and Harper told me they said. I didn't even know kids had a vocabulary like that. I told Abby and

Harper to stand up for themselves next time because bullies don't like that."

Dave had grown angry. "I can't believe kids act like this. Who teaches them to behave this way?"

Margaret sighed. "Well, the next day, they stood up for themselves when the time came, and it worked. However, the two girls told their mother that *they* were now being bullied, and guess who I received a call from yesterday?"

Dave's eyes widened. "You're kidding."

"Oh, I am *not*. I had called the school when this all started a couple weeks ago, so when their mother, Sharon, called the school to complain, they already had my account of these incidents on file. Anyway, Sharon got my number and called me. She was one of the nastiest people I've ever spoken to in my life. She was worse than the kids. She didn't want to hear a word from me, and only cared about what her two daughters told her. I hung up on her. I see where her children get their bully attitude from."

Dave sighed and leaned back in his chair. "I'm assuming you told the girls to just stay away from them for now?"

"Yes, and they'll be going to the teacher or guidance counselor anytime anything else happens, whether it's stealing or bullying. I just hope they heed my advice since I can't be there to oversee the situation."

Dave gazed toward the kitchen, watching the cooks sprinkle fresh parsley around the dishes. "Did you want me to maybe have a talk with the girls about it? I may have some good insight. I was bullied when I was in middle school. It's sort of why I got into that artistic punk scene. While trying to escape the bullies, I made friends with the 'bad boys.' Nobody messed with them, and they immediately took me in. Though I came to find out they weren't so bad, they just had that reputation."

Margaret looked to the server who was finally coming back to the table. "I think that wouldn't hurt to talk to them. They adore you, and I'm sure whatever you have to say, they will take to heart. Just don't give any bad advice, please."

Dave nodded. "Duly noted. I will definitely be mindful of what I say and how I word things. I just want them to know that this isn't the end of the world and that they will make better friends one day, especially when they get to middle school where there are loads more students to meet."

Margaret gave a sigh of relief and looked over at Dave adoringly. "You're the best."

* * *

Liz arrived home from the B&B to the smell of bread baking and tomato soup simmering. Her husband had an '80s hair metal playlist blaring, and, with an apron tied around his waist, was bent over a steaming pot, tasting the soup with a wooden spoon. He paused after the taste, thought for a minute, nodded his head in approval, then spun around with his eyes closed, fell onto his knees facing Liz, and played the air guitar like his life depended on it.

Liz let out a loud laugh, and Greg's eyes flew open, his face turning a shade of red similar to the soup.

"What on earth are you up to?" Liz asked, still laughing.

Greg got up off the floor with a big smile on his face. "I've decided to start cooking again. I let it get away from me years ago when my job became so demanding, but working from home has given me more time it seems."

Liz smiled and threw her arms around him for a big hug and kiss. "I think this is wonderful. You look so in your element. It makes me giddy to see you like this again."

Greg smiled, releasing his wife to bend down to open the oven. "Come see this. Look at how well the bread rose. Check out that golden color. I can't wait to spread that Irish butter on a slice of this bad boy tonight. That crustiness paired with the soup will be heaven."

Liz glanced at the bread and adoringly at Greg. "The old Greg I first met has somehow appeared again. The one who loved to cook and blast '80s music."

Greg laughed. "I don't know what came over me. Talking with the guys over New Year's about my Dad's old restaurant and how I've always wanted to open one has been in my head a lot lately. The wheels have been turning. It seems like since we moved to Cape May, opportunities are everywhere."

Liz grabbed his arm. "All I know is if opening a restaurant is what you want to do, then you need to figure it out and do it. I will support you."

Greg looked back over at the soup. "I've known too many people that had their restaurants go under, whether due to opening in a bad location, miscalculation of food percentages, lack of capitol when opening, or food inconsistency. It can be a very fickle business. Owners of restaurants who want it to be successful are usually there before it opens and after it closes. That kind of commitment scares me. The business demands a lot of time and attention, and I would be missing out on vacations and time with my family. Then there's the idea of only opening a small BYOB that's only open Friday through Sunday with a partner, that way we split our time there."

Liz looked over to their boys, deep in thought. "I'm sure you'll figure it out. I know you don't want to miss out on family time, but there has to be a way to have both."

Just then their sons, Michael and Steven, slid into the room on their socks like out of a movie. "Ew, what *is* this music? And please stop kissing. It's grossing us out," Michael said with his nose wrinkled.

Liz and Greg looked over at them, laughed, and kissed again while Greg cranked the volume of the music up.

Michael and Steven let out a loud sigh and slid back out of the room.

"Dinner's in an hour, boys," Greg yelled after them.

CHAPTER FOUR

A few days later, Mark had left for Germany for work, and Sarah wouldn't see him again for a month—which for a new relationship was a long time. She still wasn't sure how she felt about the situation. To not have had a serious relationship with someone for so many years, and then to get into one where she had limited time with them? It wasn't exactly what she'd waited around all these years for. It wasn't like any romance she'd ever read about.

After his surprise return home at Christmas, it felt like everything was picking up speed, but now there was this speed bump. The silent heartbreak of having her partner gone all of the time stressed her out and made her reevaluate what she wanted out of a relationship, unbeknownst to Mark. She found it hard to discuss it with him. He had been a bachelor most of his life, and going away for work was his norm. They were alike in that aspect, though. They'd both been single for many years and thriving before they met each other. Learning to adapt to someone else wasn't something either was used to.

Sarah occupied her time at her makeshift workstation at the coffeehouse among the construction workers. She felt less lonely having other people around, even if they were banging on things all day and not making much conversation. The remodel was due to finish up today, and then the scramble to clean and get the furniture and merchandise arranged would take place.

She sipped her lemon water and stared at the blueprints for the coffeehouse. She found a way to use or repurpose different parts of the bank. The vault was made to be an extra lounge area for people who wanted a quiet space, and the safety deposit boxes were part of the counter and shelving aesthetic. She hung lush green houseplants from the ceiling and positioned more of them perfectly on shelves. The bank faced the ocean, and with the huge floor-to-ceiling windows, the crashing waves were visible past the dunes. Her furniture and book orders were due to arrive later today, and everything was coming together so quickly.

Sarah shut her laptop and sat back, thinking for a moment. She slipped on her jacket and scarf and put her things into her bag, having decided it was time to go meet her neighbors. Her coffeehouse was among a big strip of stores, after all.

She stopped in at the little pottery place first, walking through an old door with little bells that chimed as she pushed it open. The adorable shop had new age music playing and a rather sweet smell permeated the space.

She noticed a woman in her early fifties standing on a step stool in the back assembling a Valentine's Day display.

"Hi, I'm Sarah. I thought I'd introduce myself since I'm going to be your new business neighbor."

The woman thought for a moment. "Oh, you mean next door at the bank? How lovely. I've noticed construction going on over there. My name is Jess by the way. I've been here for a few years now. It's a wonderful spot in town to run a business with the beach right across the street."

Sarah smiled and looked down at a pitcher that was for sale. "I'm so excited. It's been a dream of mine to open a coffeehouse, especially in my hometown. I'm so grateful I get to restore that beautiful bank."

Jess finished hanging the wooden heart banner, stepped down off the step stool, and began restocking the candle display. "Well, that's just wonderful. I wish you luck, though business has been pretty slow for a lot of us on this strip lately. Did you know this street has a coffee shop already? It's been here forever, though. They look about your age. It might be worth a trip to pick their brain."

"Perfect, I'll stop over there next. It was nice meeting you. I'll see you around," Sarah said as she stepped out of the store and walked down to the little cafe on the corner. She budged the door open to Cape Cafe and stepped inside to the aroma of coffee beans.

"Hello. I'm Sarah, your new neighbor at the old bank," she said to the couple behind the counter over the somewhat loud easy listening music.

"Oh, hi! We're Jen and Jon. What are you putting in that old bank? It's been abandoned for years. We were so happy to see someone was doing something with it *finally*."

Sarah looked around the cafe. It was very tiny. There were only a couple tables to sit at. It looked more like a place where you got your coffee to go, very different from what she was going to offer.

"Well, I'm putting in a coffeehouse. It will also have some books for sale and little areas to work and drink. I'm not sure how I missed that there was already one on this street. I guess I thought this was a little eatery."

Jen furrowed her brow. "Interesting. Well, I sure hope you don't put us out of business."

Jon nudged Jen annoyed. "Now, don't say that, Jen. We've had our regulars here for years and cater to the vegan crowd— we're the only cafe in Cape May that does that. Plus, her coffeehouse sounds very different than what we have going on here."

Jen's cheeks flushed red, probably from embarrassment. "I'm sorry, my anxiety got the best of me. We've just had a very big drop in sales this year from last. About forty percent. We're just a little worried about the business as it is."

Sarah nodded, slightly concerned herself. "I totally understand. Well, here's hoping business will pick up."

Jon leaned on the counter. "Would you like our specialty vegan Valentine's Day latte special? I promise you'll love it even if you aren't a vegan. It's on the house."

"Oh, most definitely. That sounds delicious."

Jon grabbed a cup and went to town, adding some ground chocolate and a little cherry juice before finishing it off with coconut whipped cream and tiny red candy hearts on top. He passed the steamy drink over to Sarah with a twinkle in his eyes.

Jen smiled. "Well, don't just stand there. Take a sip and let us know what you think."

Sarah took a breath before taking a sip of the beautiful drink. "Wow. This is out-of-this-world good. Like, *really* good. I've never had anything like it before."

Jon laughed. "Thank you. I concocted that one myself."

Sarah took another delightful gulp, making sure to wipe the whipped cream off her lip. "Well, I'd better get back to the bank and get to work. I'm hoping to open by the end of the month. I'd love for you guys to come see it."

Jen put her arm around Jon. "We surely will."

* * *

Margaret and Liz worked the morning shift at the B&B and were busy decorating for Valentine's Day. They'd put out some red heart doilies in the kitchen and living room, added some red tapered candles in the brass holders, and set out bowls of heart-shaped chocolates. They were a little late decorating with everything going on, as it was only a week away. There was a knock on the door, and Liz answered it with her hair in her eyes and melted chocolate all over her hands. She'd barely gotten a word out when she saw who it was.

"Is Katherine here?" William Hansen asked, looking dapper in his long black peacoat, plaid scarf, and black fedora hat.

Liz stood staring at him, starstruck. Margaret walked up beside her sister and put an arm around Liz's shoulders.

"William. What a lovely surprise. This is my sister, Liz. Don't mind her as she picks her jaw up off the ground. I'm Margaret. We're the owners of this B&B. I see you're staying next door at The Morning Dew Cottage."

William laughed. "Yes, I am. Also, no need to be starry-eyed over lil ol' me. I'm just a regular guy."

Liz finally found her voice and looked up at him with a sparkle in her eye. "Regular ol' guy? Please don't downplay yourself, sir. You are one of the greatest actors of our time. You've won three Academy Awards, for Pete's sake."

William blushed. "Ah, gee, thanks. I guess those awards were something special, huh?"

Margaret smiled. "You asked about Katherine. We don't see her much, but I think she probably is here."

Just then, Katherine came down the stairs looking like she'd slept in makeup and heels. It was 9 a.m. and she already had on bright red lipstick, a black pencil skirt, fire engine red heels, and a fitted crisp-white collared shirt that showed just the right amount of skin to make any man quiver.

"William! Come over here," Katherine said as she stood at the bottom of the stairs.

William smiled, walked over, and gave Katherine a peck on the cheek. "My, oh my. You look as beautiful as ever, Katherine Duffield. Remember that Academy Awards after-party eleven years ago? You wore that stunning red dress and sang sitting on that old grand piano? You're still just as stunning today. I've always wondered if we'd work together again, and it's *finally* happened."

Katherine blushed. "Maybe we can go talk somewhere a little more private," she said while glancing at Liz and Margaret, who'd been watching the whole exchange. They were in disbelief that this woman suddenly changed into a somewhat warm person. So far, she had only appeared cold, self-absorbed, and demanding—which turned them off a bit, frankly.

William unraveled his scarf. "That sounds good. What were you thinking?"

Margaret called up the stairs, "Katie! Can you come here please?"

Katie poked her head out into the hallway, fixed her hair, and smoothed her shirt before coming down to meet Katherine. "Hi, Katherine. Hi, William. How can I be of assistance?"

Katherine looked over at Liz and Margaret, who were already walking into the kitchen after taking their cue to leave. "Is there anywhere private William and I can hang and talk that's not a bedroom?"

Katie thought for a moment. "Well, I heard from Dolly and Kim that there's a home theater in the basement. Would that suffice for now?"

Katherine's eyes lit up. "A home theater? Oh, that would be lovely."

Liz and Margaret rolled their eyes as they entered the kitchen. The home theater was supposed to be *their* private space. It appeared they'd forgotten to mention that tiny detail to Dolly and Kim.

Katie walked into the kitchen to where Liz and Margaret were standing. "Um ... so ... can Margaret and William use the home theater?"

Margaret thought for a moment. "That's fine. We just have to quickly spruce it up."

Katie sighed in relief. She then discretely rolled her eyes

35

and mouthed, *Thank you*, knowing full well that Katherine was a pain in the butt.

Just then, a short woman with long curly blonde hair wrapped up in a red bandana hurried into the room, tripping loudly on the fallen groceries that had rolled out of the grocery bags she was holding.

Katie laughed. "Have you two met Maria yet? She's Katherine's personal chef, the one I told you about. Maria, this is Liz and Margaret, the owners of the B&B."

Maria flung a fallen potato over her shoulder into the sink, wiped the sweat off of her brow, and took off her large plaid flannel shirt, wrapping it around her waist. "Oh! How lovely. I love my room upstairs. Your place is dreamy, right by the ocean and all. I hope I won't be in your way too much. I'm going to be down here cooking up a storm. I'm also the personal chef to Diana Langston. You know her, right? I was on her movie shoot right before I got here."

"Wait. Diana Langston? I love her movies. How neat is that to be working for her?" Margaret said, astonished.

Maria blew up towards the stray curl that laid across her face, moving it out of her eyes. "Let me tell you, she is a just a *doll.* One of the nicest celebrities out there."

Liz and Margaret made a little chuckle.

Maria understood right away what they were laughing at and nodded in silent agreement. "OK, then! I'd better get to work. Ms. Katherine will probably want some snacks."

Margaret and Liz went down to the basement to clean up, and afterwards, Katherine and William made their way down to the home theater, shutting the door behind them.

Katherine marveled at the drive-in-movie style of the home theater, with the ceiling made out to be like a starry night sky and the old movie posters adorning the walls. She flicked her heels off and fell onto the couch, feeling relieved to finally have a space away from the bedroom that she could feel safe in.

"I feel like a little kid down here. I haven't been to a drive-in movie since I was a child," Katherine said, admiring the beauty of the room.

William took off his coat, sat a seat over from her, and looked the room up and down. "You're right. I've never seen a home theater look like this. It does have a special nostalgia about it."

Katherine smiled. "You know, it was the drive-in movies that really made me want to be an actor. I have such fond memories of going with my grandparents. They always supported my dreams of being on the screen. They didn't get to live long enough to see me do it, though."

William's eyes softened. "I'm sure they would be so proud of what you've become."

Katherine reclined back on the couch, kicking her feet up onto the ottoman. "Thank you, William. I appreciate that." She paused and looked back up at the starry ceiling. "Gee, I wonder if they have any old classic movies down here. I'd love to watch one just like we did at the drive-in theater."

William walked over to the DVD case. "Here's one right in the front that I think you'll like. I'll get it playing."

Katherine spotted the old popcorn machine and walked over to inspect it. "Look! I think this popcorn machine works. There's already popcorn kernels in it. I'm going to see what happens when I press start."

Moments later, the popcorn machine having warmed up, began to make loud popping noises as the kernels pinged against the walls of the old vintage machine. The nostalgic popcorn smell permeated the room, and William dimmed the lights as the movie started to play.

Katherine smiled, feeling happy for the first time in months.

* * *

Upstairs, Maria turned on her upbeat music and prepared some snacks for Katherine while Margaret and Liz walked into the living room and plopped into some chairs, feeling a little exhausted from the day already.

Maria popped her head into the living room. "Hey, you two. Are you hungry? Can I cook you something?"

"Well, we don't want to overstep our boundaries since you're here for Katherine," Liz said, though she felt very hungry.

Maria scoffed. "Nonsense. As long as I'm here, you two have things to eat. I will make sure of it. Don't worry about Katherine."

Margaret thought about all of the demands Katherine had. "I don't know. I don't have a good feeling about this."

Maria let out an aggressive sigh and threw the towel in her hand on the ground. "Let's all step out front for a moment."

Margaret and Liz looked at each other, confused, but followed Maria outside to the porch.

Maria pulled a bruised pepper out of her pocket, looked it at it, and chucked it into the bushes, then spoke in a hushed tone. "Don't be afraid of Katherine. Do not let her make you feel like she's superior to you, and by all means, *do not* treat her any differently than anyone else. I know about her list of demands. I've seen her riders on past jobs. They are ridiculous. I've been her personal chef for twenty years now, and she knows I don't put up with any of her shenanigans, so she doesn't pull those kinds of demands on me. I cook for her and that's it, unless I offer to do something else, and she knows it. She once tried to get me to drive her somewhere when I first started working for her. I flat out told her no. She's never asked me to do anything else besides cook since then. I have a waitlist of celebrity clients, and she knows it."

Liz chuckled, loving Maria already. "Well, what about the don't-look-her-in-the-eyes requirement?"

Maria let loose a laugh loud enough to be heard down the

block. "Did they really tell you that? Wow, her demands have gotten worse and worse. I haven't seen or heard what they are these days."

Margaret looked out towards the paparazzi who were across the street, camped out in cars and on the sidewalk. "I appreciate you telling us this, but we don't want to upset her while she's here."

Maria shook her head. "You know, she wasn't always like this. This diva routine started as soon as the peak in her acting career was over. Have you noticed she hasn't been in many movies lately? I'm not a psychologist, but I think she started making more demands as a way to make herself feel important when her acting roles began to decline. Then there was the car accident ten years ago... but we won't discuss that now. Anyway, what can I make you? How about my roasted red pepper hummus, with some vegetables and pita?"

Liz smiled. "Yes, that sounds wonderful. Thank you."

Margaret chuckled. "I'm starving. I'll take whatever you give us at this point."

Maria cocked her head to the side. "Oh, really? I've got a few other things up my sleeve for you two, then. Also, in case you didn't know, I feed everyone at this B&B, including Katherine's assistants, and anyone else who works or visits here. So don't feel like you're overstepping any boundaries.

CHAPTER FIVE

Beep. Margaret's cell phone went to voice mail.

"Hi, girls, it's your mother and father. We're still in Italy, and love it here so much. We've been figuring out the trains, and have been visiting the most awe-inspiring places. Hope everything is going well at the B&B with Katherine Duffield. Did you tell her I said hi yet? Love you two!"

Judy ended the call and walked over to where Bob, Ruth, and Bill were standing. They'd just gotten off the train and were now in Cinque Terre, an old seaside locality full of colorful villages and vineyards that sat atop a big cliff over the water. Each village connected by a hiking trail on the cliff, and their plan was to walk it today. They were all a little out of shape, but figured they would stop and rest when needed.

Bob led the way to the trail, pointing out the vibrantly colored houses. "I read these houses were painted like this so fisherman could find their homes while they were out at sea."

Ruth stopped to look out towards the ocean and looked back at the long path that awaited them. "My bunions are painful today," she said. "Do they have an easier way to walk this trail? And these flowers are making my allergies act up. How about Bill and I meet you and Judy at the last village? I'm craving onion rings with ranch. I bet we can find them at a restaurant over there." Ruth straightened her red cowboy hat. She was now the only person wearing one around Italy.

Judy rolled her eyes on the inside. "That's fine. We'll give you a call when we're nearing the end so we can meet up."

Ruth and Bill walked off, presumably to find transportation to the last village, and Bob blew out a long sigh of relief. Judy took his hand to walk down a steep set of stairs to the trail.

"Well, we dodged a bullet with that one. If I had to listen to Ruth complain about everything one more day, I was going to scream," Bob said shaking his head.

Judy laughed. "I'm right there with ya. They don't savor all of the little things like we do. You and I can just enjoy our own hike together, and maybe we'll find a place to eat along the path."

Bob laughed. "That sounds perfect. I have to say, though, while Ruth and Bill are our friends, I don't think I'll ever travel with them again. I guess you see different sides of people in different situations. They aren't immersing themselves in this wonderful Italian culture like we are. You can't expect to have everything you have at home here, and I feel like they're letting that get in the way of this wonderful experience."

Judy nodded. "I agree, but let's not let it spoil *our* time in Italy. Maybe we can start doing our own thing each day and meet them later for dinner or a walk around the city or town we're in. I have to say, even though we're married, I never knew we'd be so compatible traveling together abroad since we've never done it before. You're so easygoing, and I like to plan out itineraries. You like to just go along with whatever I plan, and it just works out so nicely. You're enjoying yourself, right? Because I sure am."

Bob leaned over and picked a pink rose from the many rose bushes up the cliff. "Yes, I am. I love it here, and I love that you plan our days—I wouldn't have a clue of where to go or what to see. This is for you, my beautiful."

Judy blushed and held the rose to her nose, breathing in deeply to enjoy its subtle scent. This trip had definitely been good for their marriage, especially when everything was starting to feel like an old routine back home. When Judy had brought up the idea of going abroad for a month or more to Bob, she'd half expected him to not be interested. He'd never been big on traveling. However, unexpectedly, he'd agreed. Not only that, he'd appeared more excited than Judy about the entire thing.

They walked the trail, taking in the sights, sounds, and smells with every step, and when they came upon a little restaurant up a set of stairs, they couldn't resist stopping. It only had three small tables outside, each with an umbrella, but the view was spectacular. Patrons had front-row seats to the sea from high above. Bob sat at the table while Judy walked inside to grab menus.

They both ordered a glass of white wine and the pesto lasagna, savoring every delicious bite, especially after the appetite they'd worked up from walking the trail.

Bob held Judy's hand as they sat and admired the grapevines and flowers, the sea, and all of the people who walked the trail together below. They embraced the feeling of peace and relaxation. Life felt like it moved at a slower place in Italy; there wasn't any rush to get anywhere. It felt like they were in control of time now, doing with it what they pleased.

In that moment, Judy received a text. She glanced at her phone and saw it was Bill.

Um … Ruth wants me to ask if you know of any place around here that might have tacos. She asked for ranch and onion rings, and the waiter looked at her like she had two heads. I don't think the red cowboy hat with a cat eating spaghetti helped the matter. Now she wants tacos. Don't ask.

Judy ignored the ridiculous message since she and Bob were in a blissful moment that she didn't want interrupted, and she turned her phone off.

"That's it. Phone's going off until we're done on the trail. I want to enjoy every moment of this without interruption."

Bob chuckled. "I'm guessing that was Ruth?"

Judy rolled her eyes. "It was poor Bill messaging me on behalf of Ruth. She now wants tacos. What country does she think she's in?"

Bob got up of out of his seat, and grabbed Judy's hand. "Come, let's go burn off our lunch on the trail."

* * *

Dave carried his tools onto the set and found himself surrounded by the loud sounds of a radio and reverberating bangs coming from every direction. The construction crew were still adding things to the interior of Katherine's character's house. In the movie, she'll have a modest house, nothing like what she's used to in real life.

"Heads up. Here's a water for you if you need it." Brad tossed a bottle of water to Dave. "I haven't seen you before. You new?"

Dave caught the bottle with one hand, unscrewed the cap, and gulped down nearly half the water. "Yep. My first day. My sister, Irene, works as a PA, and she told me you all needed some help over here. Let me know where to start."

Brad smiled. "You're *Irene's* brother. I like you already, my man. Have you built a set before?"

Dave set his half-empty water down and looked around the room. "Nope, but I do build things for a living. I'm happy to learn as I go."

Brad raised his hand out for a fist bump, which Dave obliged. "Well, perfect. I'm Brad. Glad to have you on board. Come with me, and I'll give you the rundown, then we can decide where the best place for you to start is."

Dave nodded, a rush of excitement pulsed through him that made the hair on his arms stand up. He was satisfied by the rewarding work he did at the refuge, but this kind of work was a level of excitement that he'd never been a part of. For one, he hadn't worked alongside other people in the construction profession in years, so it was nice to be part of a team again.

Brad walked among the other crew members who were busy working on the set's living room. "This is the living room, as you can see. That staircase goes nowhere, as I'm sure you already know, but Ricky has fallen off of them," Brad said as he rolled his eyes and chuckled. "He's fine. Don't worry."

Just then, a man holding his neck peeked around the corner. "I'm Ricky. Just got a little whiplash is all. Nothing that'll stop me from surfing though. You local? I hear you can catch some good waves in these parts. "

Dave chuckled. "Nice to meet you. I'm Dave. Yes, I'm a local. I used to surf all the time in my twenties—so it's been a long time—but sometimes the swells are awesome out here. You guys looking to surf?"

Brad chimed in. "Oh, yeah. We most definitely are. We'd be glad to have you come with us, and maybe show us the best spots? There's about ten of us going. You know us California guys and gals need the ocean."

A few other workers overheard the conversation and introduced themselves with some handshakes. Dave was overjoyed to be working with such a cool crew.

"I do have a favorite surfing spot from way back when. I'll have to ask around about how good it is these days. It had some fun barrels and good breaks. It probably doesn't compare to what you have in California, but it's something," Dave said while fastening his tool belt around his waist.

Ricky poked his head around again, this time rubbing his bruised arm. "Perfect. I'm stoked to get out there. Next day off, let's all get something going. Maybe grab some burritos or something beforehand to fuel up."

Brad looked over at Ricky and shook his head. "Are you

OK, my man? You seem more banged up then you've been letting on. Is your arm hurt too?"

Ricky stopped and looked down at his arm. "Oh, this old thing? It just fell asleep while I was talking to you guys. Trying to get the pins and needles out, you know what I'm saying?"

Brad rolled his eyes, not really believing that excuse. "OK, but I still think you need to go get checked out. How about I call the on-set nurse? I think she's in the trailer. I'm sure it won't take long."

Ricky sighed. "Fine. You're probably right."

Brad picked up his phone, but turned to Dave first. "I almost forgot to tell you where to start. You can finish off the windows here in the living room with me."

Right then, Irene walked in, headset on and walkie-talkie in hand. "OK. Copy that. In thirty minutes, I'll have Katherine in hair and makeup."

She removed and unplugged the headset, dragging it across her blonde locks, and turned up the walkie-talkie so she could hear any calls. "I'm so over this headset today. Hearing people call for you in your ear all day long gets super old, especially when it's *Ron*."

Brad put his hand gently on her shoulder. "Ron the assistant director? What's his deal?"

Irene looked around the room, then sighed and spoke softly. "Maybe I'll tell you about that later. He's just a little hard to work for right now."

Brad's eyes softened and he gave a frown to Irene, showing his dismay.

Irene ran her hands through her hair and removed her hoodie, tying it around her waist. "I'm so hot from running around all day. I haven't even had a second to take this hoodie off until now."

"Well, you're always welcome to use the construction area as your safe space," Brad said, smiling at Irene.

Irene took a long gulp of her water bottle. "Thanks, Brad. I appreciate it."

Brad pointed to Dave who was working on the window with another crew member. "Did you see Dave was here? He's a cool guy. He's already jumped right in before I could even show him anything, and he's going surfing with us."

Dave looked over, hearing his name, and waved at Irene.

Irene smiled. "Hey, Dave! They treating you OK so far?" Dave nodded in affirmation. "Lunch is in about an hour. Hope you're hungry, the catering trucks are phenomenal on this shoot. They must have had a good budget for it."

"Everyone's been super cool so far. Thanks for getting me on this," Dave said while working.

Irene sighed and jumped off the set platform. "I guess I'll go find Ron."

Brad scrunched his eyebrow. "Do you want to go for a quick walk with me? Need to vent? You don't look too happy. I'm fine to take a ten-minute break since I'm the only one who hasn't taken one yet."

Irene thought for a moment. "That would be nice. I still have some time before I have to get Katherine. Let's go this way, away from base camp."

Brad jumped off the platform and walked up beside her. "So, what's going on?"

Once they made it out of earshot, Irene took a deep breath. "Well, Ron doesn't let me have a second of downtime, even though he gets plenty of it. If I even try to stop and take a swig of my water bottle, go to the bathroom, or grab a snack from craft service, he jumps down my throat. He says things like 'You'll never move up to an AD if you're not hustling hard enough.' One time, I went to the bathroom and when I got out he was like, 'Where were you? We needed you. Why didn't you answer your walkie?' Meanwhile, I had told him I was going to the bathroom, and *he* didn't have his walkie on."

Brad shook his head. "Being a production assistant is

rough. Trust me, I know because I was one for years until switching to the construction side of things. You're expected to give your all for little pay with very long hours. Heck, I remember the production assistants weren't even allowed to eat at the catering location when it was meal break. Instead, we were assigned fire watch on all of the film equipment outside while the rest of the crew got to eat comfortably at the tables and chairs in the heated or air-conditioned venue. It's a thankless job, and that's why so many don't last."

Irene nodded in agreement. "Oh, I know. Most of the time, I love this job. I love working with the actors, being on set among my coworkers who are all friends, and being a part of the making of a great film, but then there're days like this, where I'm working under a drill sergeant assistant director without a lick of empathy."

Brad gave her a playful nudge with his shoulder. "Well, you can talk to me anytime about it. I'm always here," he said with a smile while holding her gaze a little longer than normal.

Irene blushed and turned her crystal-blue eyes towards the faint sounds of the crashing waves a couple blocks away. "Thank you. I just can't wait to move on from being a PA. It's crazy that I left a job that required at least half the hours but more than doubled the pay all because I wanted to start anew after a bad breakup. Was I crazy?"

Brad thought for a moment. "No. I think you did what was best for you at the time. I am going to advise you to keep your options open, though. Maybe you'll decide to stay in the film business but move to a different department like myself. I asked to be moved onto the construction team, and I was brought on, thankfully. It's a whole other world in this department. We have much more freedom, better pay, and overall, higher job satisfaction. I don't think I would have been happy as an assistant director, but that's just me. Maybe you'll decide to get out of the film business altogether. Who knows. You're young still. Just do what makes you the happiest."

Irene laughed. "Young? I'm nearly forty. You're too kind. I'm so glad we had this talk. What would I do without you?"

Brad smiled and started to reply but stopped, fearing it would be too bold to flirt in the moment. "Well, you don't have to wonder since I'm right here."

Irene stopped and looked at Brad. Though she wanted to hug him for significantly helping to lighten up her mood, she felt shy about it. "I guess I'll go find Katherine now. I'm starving, I can't wait for lunch. I heard they're doing Mediterranean today, all cooked from scratch."

Brad rubbed his stomach. "Yum. Maybe I'll see you at lunch," he said with a wink and a smile.

Irene turned and started back toward the trailers with a smile plastered on her face. She had a funny feeling that there was some mutual unsaid feelings going on between the two of them, and that made her heart flutter. She hadn't dated anyone or been interested in anyone since her ex, deciding to focus on herself first. She somehow felt ready now, though.

CHAPTER SIX

Thousands of red rose petals lay scattered on the walkway up to The Seahorse Inn, and Margaret and Liz were unsure where they'd come from. Had Dave or Greg done it? Maybe a fan of Katherine's?

It was Valentine's Day, and a huge snowstorm was due later, so the producers decided to halt production until the storm passed through. That meant it was a crowded house at the B&B as everyone hunkered down.

Margaret had just lit the fireplace and the red tapered candles on the mantle when there was a knock at the door. She answered to see Irene with a stack of papers in her hands.

"Hey, Margaret. How are things here? I've been so busy that I haven't had a chance to come by much," Irene said flipping through the papers.

"Hi, Irene. Things have been good. Do you want to come inside?" Margaret said as she opened the door wider for Irene.

Irene ripped off her headset and placed the stack down on a side table by the door. "Thank you. That would be great. I have some call sheets for Katherine and her assistants before I head back to my room to settle in. They just outline the shooting schedule for when filming resumes. They expect that to be two days from now, figuring all the streets will be plowed by then, but we'll see. I hear this storm is going to be the worst this area has seen in years."

Liz walked out from the kitchen after overhearing the conversation. "I just heard the same thing. They're calling for over two feet of snow. It's kind of crazy but exciting. I love the snow."

Irene looked towards the kitchen. "Is Maria here? Katherine's personal chef? I'd love to chat with her. We've gotten to know each other over the past couple of years."

Maria poked her head from the kitchen. "Irene? Get over here and give me a hug!"

Irene joyfully rushed across the room to give Maria a hug. "It's so good to see you. How's everything been?"

Maria fixed the bandana on her head, walked back into the kitchen with Irene on her heels, and turned up her music while doing a little shimmy around the room, tossing vegetables into a strainer to be washed. "Oh, it's been great. Just cooking for the stars, per usual. Do you want to stay for dinner?"

"Oh, I couldn't. I don't want to impose. Plus, does Katherine really want me hanging around for dinner?" Irene said looking around to make sure nobody was listening.

Maria stopped abruptly and cocked her head to the side. "You're staying for dinner. End of story."

Maria was very straightforward and a tad bit bossy, but in a good way. She always wanted to include everyone, even if she was pushy about it. She meant well, though.

Margaret and Liz walked into the kitchen to straighten up for the meal. "What are you cooking up tonight, Maria?" Liz asked while trying to peek at what was all over the island counter.

"Well, Katherine has asked for sushi. I'm making a ton of it, as well as some homemade miso soup and champagne with strawberries. I'm assuming you two will be staying for dinner as well? If not, why *not?*"

Liz cleared her throat. "That dinner sounds amazing, but I have to get home to my family."

Maria threw a sweet potato into the air and promptly caught it. "Nonsense! Just stay for dinner. I've made so much, and I need more people to feed."

Margaret smiled. "We'll stay for dinner. Sounds lovely. We should be able to make it home before the storm. My girls are with Liz's husband and kids tonight, so we should be OK, right?" Margaret said while looking at Liz.

Liz smiled. "You're right. Plus, I'm dying for sushi. I can eat a few quickly."

Maria clapped her hands together. "Great! Wait until you try my sushi. It's very good. I made vegetarian sushi, too, so something for everyone."

"Maria, do you know anything about all these rose petals on the walkway and porch? Did you see who did it?" Margaret asked.

Maria thought for a moment. "Well, I have an idea of who did it, but that's all I'm going to say about that. Everyone get comfortable and pour yourself a drink."

Just then, there was a knock at the front door and Margaret opened it to see Sarah holding some bags of coffee beans and books.

"Sarah, so good to see you. Come inside."

Sarah smiled as she walked in, hearing Maria's music and inhaling the delicious smell coming from the kitchen. "My coffeehouse is coming along quicker than I anticipated. It's looking like I'll be able to open it next week, a week earlier than anticipated. I wanted to come by and drop off some of my roasted coffee beans and a few books I thought you, Liz, and the kids might like.."

Margaret grabbed the items graciously with widened eyes. "You're kidding. That's excellent. Did you hear, Liz?"

Liz walked out of the kitchen, that was full of laughs and upbeat music, holding a glass of champagne with two ripe strawberries bobbing in it. "Well, if it isn't Miss Sarah. Did I hear you're opening next week? I can't wait to be the first in line. I'm so excited to see it. Come meet Maria in the kitchen. Irene, Dave's sister who you met last year, is also here."

Maria exited the kitchen, wiping her hands on the hand towel she had draped over her shoulder. "Who is this? Well, that doesn't matter—do you like sushi? Come sit with us."

Margaret laughed. "This is Sarah, one of our oldest and dearest friends. She's about to open up a local coffeehouse."

"You're kidding. I owned a coffee shop once years and years ago. Come make yourself comfortable in the kitchen," Maria said leading the way.

Margaret followed behind, placing the beautiful array of coffee beans and books in the middle of the table.

They all sat at the kitchen table, relaxing with some drinks and laughing while Irene and Maria took turns telling hilarious stories of working on film sets or with celebrities when Katherine suddenly appeared at the opening to the kitchen. Katherine normally ate upstairs, away from everyone.

Immediately, the room grew quiet, except for Maria who was shimmying her way to the kitchen table with enormous platters of sushi.

"Katherine! Are you hungry? It's just about ready," Maria said while looking over at her.

Katherine looked at everyone in the room. "Why did you all stop talking when I arrived? Please continue talking and laughing. I came down because of all the lively chatter down here. I love stories from the film sets. I could chime in with a bunch of my own."

Irene immediately jumped up and pulled a chair out for her. "Did you want to sit here?"

Katherine, wearing a red blouse and jeans, slowly made her way over. "Thank you, Irene. I was just so bored of being in my room, and I heard all of this laughter down here. I could use some of it since it's the tenth anniversary of my car accident. It's the one day of the year I don't look forward to, and oddly enough, it falls on Valentine's Day."

Liz and Margaret sat stunned, shocked even. They'd been told not to talk to Katherine or look her in the eye. She hadn't been the nicest or most social person they'd ever met. They weren't sure what to do.

Margaret, not wanting to pry, spoke up. "Well, it's nice to have you here with us. Please join in if you'd like. Maybe we can make this day a little happier for you. I know the anniversary of a car accident probably brings up painful memories."

Katherine nodded and rested her chin in her hands. "Things just haven't been the same since that awful day. It affected me and my career greatly. I became too scared to drive or be driven anywhere. I had to turn down film roles—big ones, at that. Ones that went on to produce Oscar winners for best lead and supporting actress. My career took a nosedive as well as my mental health … but that's a story for another day."

Just then, Katie and Erin arrived. "Katherine. Didn't expect to see you here. Can we get you something?" Katie asked as she looked worriedly around the room at everyone.

Katherine smiled. "I'm fine. I chose to come down here. I couldn't bear to sit upstairs any longer."

Maria motioned to the table while dancing and chopping chocolate for the dessert. "Sit. I'm about to serve dinner. Pour yourselves some champagne."

Erin and Katie, rather reluctantly took seats and poured themselves a drink.

Margaret cleared her throat. "Well, while I have everyone here. Does anyone know who threw those rose petals on the walkway outside and up onto the porch?"

Katherine's eyes widened, and she immediately got up to go look, walking out of the kitchen and opening the front door to get a better view. The cold air hit her hard, making her cheeks and nose turn rosy red, almost the same color as her hair. "William," she said to herself with a smile.

She stepped out onto the porch, hugging herself and rubbing her arms, while looking out towards the ocean, hearing the loud, angry waves crashing down. She noticed an outdoor light pop on next door at The Morning Dew Cottage and looked over to see William step outside bundled up in his peacoat, scarf, and hat. He hadn't seen her standing there as he walked down the driveway and over to The Seahorse Inn holding a bouquet of roses. Katherine waited on the porch, her heart racing.

William made his way to the top of the steps, placing the bouquet of roses in Katherine's hands while giving her a soft peck on the cheek. "Happy Valentine's Day, Katherine," he said softly enough so no one else could hear. Luckily, the paparazzi were nowhere to be found due to the impending storm.

Katherine raised the roses to her nose and inhaled, taking in their subtle scent. "Thank you, William. I should say the same to you. Come inside and have dinner with us."

William walked inside, divested himself of his hat and coat, and rubbed his hands together for warmth while following Katherine into the kitchen.

Everyone in the room was still talking, drinking, and laughing, but turned to see William standing there in the flesh—the man they'd all had a crush on at one point or another.

Maria dimmed the lights, lit the candles on the table, and put together another setting for William. "Great to see you, William. I've got a spot right here next to Katherine for you."

William looked around the room with a sparkle in his eyes. "I've never had a Valentine's dinner with so many ladies at once. The sushi looks exquisite, Maria."

Everyone gave a giddy laugh and welcomed him to the table, trying not stare, except Margaret, who was deep in thought. She sighed and looked over at Liz. "I haven't heard from Dave all day. I wonder what he's up to. Are they still working on the set?"

Katherine turned to Margaret as she held a vegetarian sushi roll with her chopsticks. "Dave? As in the one who's building my set house?"

Margaret, still unsure if she was allowed to make direct eye contact, turned to look at her. "Yep, that's him. Have you met him?"

Katherine dipped her sushi in the soy sauce and wasabi. "I haven't, but I hear very good things about him. I visited the set and could see that he and the rest of the crew have been doing a fantastic job. Call him and tell him to come over for sushi. Maria made enough for an army."

Maria chimed in. "Yes, call him now."

Margaret smiled, grabbed her phone, and walked out onto the porch for privacy. She called, but it went straight to voice mail. It was very odd that she hadn't heard a peep from him all day, especially on this particular day. It was their first Valentine's together. Her heart sank in her chest as she started to ponder why he hadn't called. She looked out towards the ocean and down the street one more time before turning to go back inside, when suddenly a figure appeared on the street. He was jogging. She watched as he jogged straight to the front gates of The Seahorse Inn. It was Dave.

Margaret walked out to meet him at the driveway, holding her arms around herself to keep warm as she'd not put a coat on.

Without saying a word Dave threw his arms around her and gave her a kiss.

Margaret felt her heart rise again. "Where have you been all day? I was getting a little worried."

Dave sighed. "They had us change a few things in the bathroom of Katherine's home before the storm hits, and my phone died and of course my charger was at home. I felt so horrible. I couldn't wait to get over here, to be with you."

Margaret hugged him again, clasping her arms around his waist, letting his open jacket wrap around her for warmth.

"Well, we're all inside having a big Valentine's dinner together. You're invited," Margaret said with a smile.

Dave followed her inside. "Who exactly is 'we all'?"

Margaret laughed. "Oh, you'll find out soon enough."

As Dave followed her, he grabbed her hand one last time before they walked inside. "After dinner, I want you to come to the set with me before the storm really hits. I want to show you something."

They walked back inside where the cacophony of laughter, talking, and music welcomed them. Maria's colorful and delicate sushi rolls had taken over the table, and she was just starting to ladle the homemade miso soup into bowls, passing them out one by one.

Dave's eyes widened when he walked into the kitchen, not expecting to see the two big Hollywood stars eating at the table.

"Come take a seat, Dave," Katherine said as she graciously took the bowl of miso soup from Maria.

Dave smiled, said his hellos, and joined everyone in a delightful night of conversation and food.

After dinner, Liz got up from the table as Maria was serving chocolate cake. "I'd love to stay, but I need to get home to my family. They just got home from indoor soccer practice, so it works out perfectly. Thank you for everything, Maria, and thank you all for that wonderful dinner and chat."

Sarah stood up right after Liz. "I have to get home, too. Mark and I have a video call date tonight that I'm excited about. He's been so busy on this work trip abroad, we've barely gotten to talk much. Everyone enjoy the coffee and books on the table."

Dave took Liz and Sarah leaving and Dolly and Kim arriving for their evening shift as his cue. He looked over at

Margaret and smiled. "Is now a good time for us to walk over?"

"Now is perfect," Margaret said as she took a last bite of the decadent chocolate cake before standing from her seat. "Let's go now before the snow really starts to stick."

They grabbed their coats, scarves, and hats, and walked over to the set that Dave had been building. It was in an old abandoned warehouse a few blocks down the road and Dave had the key to the door. The snow had just started floating around them, landing softly on their hair and coats.

Dave unlocked the door, turned some lights on, and gently grabbed Margaret's hand, leading her to the living room set.

"Wow. You guys did some amazing work here. I love all of the attention to detail, even down to the curtains," Margaret said as she walked around the set.

Dave smiled. "Yeah, it's been so fun to work on this with the rest of the crew. Did you know that Margaret and William have a romantic slow dance scene right here where I'm standing in the living room?"

He played a slow love song on his phone and motioned for Margaret to come over with his finger and a sneaky grin.

Margaret blushed and walked over, then they danced to the entire song together. "This is so romantic. To dance together on this set that you built just like Katherine and William will do in a scene."

The song ended and Dave walked across the room to a package wrapped in newspaper and tied up with a red ribbon. "Oh yeah, I've got a gift for you."

"Oh, my. I didn't bring your gift. It's back at my house. I wanted to wait until we were alone," Margaret said as she started unwrapping it. She gasped when she saw it.

Dave walked over next to her to look over her shoulder at it. "It's a painting of the farm stand. The Cape May Garden. I thought it was something you'd like to have."

Before Dave could get another word out, Margaret hurtled

herself at him for a tight hug. "I love it. I absolutely love it. That farm stand was what brought us together, and what brought me out of hard times during my divorce. I miss it terribly right now since it's winter. It's the best gift I could've possibly asked for."

As they turned the lights off, locked up, and started back to the inn, they saw Brad walking up towards them. "Hey, guys," he said.

"Hey, Brad. Heading back to set?" Dave asked.

"I left my phone and decided to come back for it," Brad said, looking exhausted.

Dave gave him a fist bump and looked towards the ocean. "We're heading back to The Seahorse Inn. Katherine is staying there, and this is Margaret, she owns the B&B with her sister."

Margaret looked over at Brad. "Irene, Katherine, William, and the rest of the gang are there. There's still a ton of sushi left. Would you want to stop by and join us?"

Brad's eyes lit up. "Irene is there? That's interesting. Yeah, I think I'll stop by."

Margaret chuckled to herself and nudged Dave. They both looked at each other and winked. Surely Brad had a thing for Irene, as he seemed more interested in going because she was there rather than the two celebrities.

The storm had dropped about an inch of snow on the ground already, and it was coming down hard as they made their way back to the B&B.

Once they got to the porch, Margaret pointed the way inside to Brad before turning back to Dave. "Would you want to close out Valentine's Day with me and the girls? I'm going to go pick them up at Liz and Greg's, then watch a movie and do a little craft with them."

Dave smiled and looked back over at his truck on the street. "Most definitely. I have a few gifts for them as well. I'll meet you over there."

Just as Margaret got to her car, her phone dinged with a text message to her and Dave from Irene.

I don't know how you two did it, but thank you for bringing Brad over. He seems genuinely excited to be here, and he was starving. Maria just put a plate full of sushi in front of him. Katherine and William invited all of us to watch some old movies in the basement home theater. It's definitely a memorable Valentine's Day. I love you two.

CHAPTER SEVEN

A week later, Sarah stood in her now completely finished coffeehouse early in the morning before opening day. She walked around the grand old space, admiring every little detail. The weathered wood beams on the ceiling drew attention to the shabby chic crystal chandeliers that hung low enough to be seen upon stepping inside. She strolled behind the counter and gazed at the coffee roasting machine, picking up one of the many bags of coffee beans, she opened it and breathed in the smell. It made her smile. Her newly hired staff would be arriving shortly, and the doors would finally open to the abandoned bank turned coffeehouse by the sea.

The glass case by the register was stocked with fresh local pastries, and some shelves and tables around the store overflowed with captivating and colorful book covers. With her counseling skills guiding her, she'd arranged some quiet sections of chairs and couches that would help invoke peace, calm, and happiness to those who needed a sanctuary away from crowds. The new space also featured some dog-friendly areas off to the side, away from everyone else. The floor-to-ceiling windows let in wonderful sunlight and gave a glimpse of the sand dunes and ocean across the street. The place had come together beautifully.

Just then, Margaret arrived at the front door and gawked at beauty of the place. "This is amazing, Sarah. I can't believe you're finally opening today."

Sarah gave a forced smile and slumped into one of the many chairs in the room. "Thank you. It really is nice, isn't it?"

Margaret sensed something was wrong right away. "Are you OK?"

Sarah placed her head back on the cushion of the couch and stared at the high ceiling. "I broke up with Mark last night. It's just not working with him being away for his job so much. And here I am opening up my dream business, and I'm too sad to enjoy it."

Shocked, Margaret walked over to Sarah and plopped next to her on the couch. "I'm so sorry. Do you need anything? Can I help in any way?"

Sarah pulled a tissue out of her purse and blew her nose while tears welled in her eyes. "No, I think I'm fine. I just think the relationship was taking a toll on me. I've been single for so many years waiting for the right man to come along, and this is what I've been waiting for? A man who's barely ever around? The relationship still made me feel single, honestly."

Margaret gave a sympathetic frown. "How did Mark take it?"

"Not well. He understood where I was coming from, but he was quite upset. We've both been single for many years, and I think we're each used to how certain things in our lives already were before we met. I don't think he took into consideration how his job would affect our relationship, and neither did I," Sarah said, getting up to walk behind the counter. She grabbed an enormous cupcake with a sugared flower on top and took a huge bite.

Margaret stood there, not sure of what to say next. Sarah was obviously out of sorts. It was 6 a.m. and she was noshing on a cupcake. "Well, maybe you can busy your mind with the coffeehouse opening. Think of all the wonderful customers that will come in today and of the many ways your new business will flourish."

Sarah took another bite. "That's the other thing. Cape Cafe, the cafe down the street told me that their business is down forty percent from last year. That scares me, Margaret. I'm afraid I've gotten myself into a mess. What if nobody shows up today?"

Margaret walked over to the door and gazed out towards the ocean. "Honestly, Sarah, this place is phenomenal. It's cozy, beautiful, *and* it's right by the beach. I have a feeling you'll do just fine. Maybe your business will help the cafe down the street too."

Sarah furrowed her brow. "How so? I thought I'd only be their competition. They seemed a little concerned at first when I told them I was opening a coffeehouse, but they were the sweetest people. I don't want to cause any issues for them."

Margaret picked up a nearby book and flipped through the pages. "I think by you bringing in more foot traffic, it will also draw more business for them. You can support each other, differentiate yourselves. How is Cape Cafe different from your coffeehouse?"

Sarah smiled. "I guess you're right. We're very different."

Margaret made her way back to the door, wrapping her scarf around her neck. "There you go. Their cafe has been around a while too, right? They probably already have a big customer base, and you have to start fresh. I think it will all work out in the end. I have to get over to the B&B. Luckily, I can hang out in the home theater while I work my full-time job at the wildlife refuge."

Sarah threw her hair up into a ponytail. "I can't believe you're still full-time at the wildlife refuge while running the B&B. You must be so busy and burnt out."

Margaret thought for a moment. "Pretty much, but I end

up being able to work from the B&B, and we have hired help now. I am thinking about asking to go part time, though. Oh yeah, what's the name of your coffeehouse?"

Sarah laughed. "I kind of decided the name super last minute, which is why the sign isn't up outside yet. It's called Monarch Coffee, in honor of all the monarch butterflies that stop in Cape May on their way to Mexico in the fall. The sign will have a big monarch butterfly on it. Did you notice all of the subtle butterflies through the shop?"

Margaret glanced around the room, now noticing pops of orange and black from the monarch's wings peeking out from the shelves up high, the book displays, and near the counter. "Wow. You sure made that beautiful and subtle. I absolutely love it."

* * *

Liz and Greg sat at a table at their favorite restaurant, Bistro Fiorelli in Philadelphia, for an early dinner, taking in the sights and sounds. It was an old remodeled Italian restaurant with a wine cellar in the basement that also held tables and booths to dine at, which is where they were seated. The restaurant kept the cellar dimly lit, the candles at the tables gave a romantic glow and added rustic ambiance. A server came by holding a bottle of pinot noir.

"Two glasses, please," Greg said as he looked over at Liz with a smile.

The server poured the wine and Liz took a sip, gazing at a dish of calamari that passed by in another server's hands. "I love being here. So glad you came up with this idea."

Greg smiled. "Well, there's a reason I wanted to come here. I'm doing research on the restaurant I want to open. While I don't want to duplicate this restaurant, I'm greatly inspired by it, especially this cellar area."

Liz laughed. "Why didn't you tell me that's why we were coming here?"

"I don't know. I was afraid you wouldn't want to come if I told you that," Greg said while looking down at the menu.

Liz scrunched her brow. "Of course I'd want to come. I support your dream of opening a restaurant, remember?"

Greg looked over the menu at Liz with a smirk. "Good, because there's a property in Cape May that I have booked for us to look at later today."

Liz laughed. "Perfect. Can't hurt to start getting some ideas, right?"

The server arrived back to deliver their appetizer, burrata with baked butternut squash and an olive oil drizzle with crusty homemade bread.

Greg leaned over the dish, taking in the sweet and savory smells steaming off of it and looked over at the server. "I think we're ready to order our entrees. Go ahead, Liz."

"I'm going to have the gnocchi with white-and-black truffle cream."

Greg eyed the menu one last time with a big smile. "And I'm going to have the roasted chicken dish with Brussels."

The server nodded, took their menus, and walked over to the next table over.

Liz took another gulp of wine. "So, what have you been cooking up in that brain of yours for this restaurant idea?"

Greg clasped his hands together and cracked his knuckles, just waiting for this moment. "Well, I want to do an Italian and seafood restaurant that's only open Thursday through Saturday or Sunday, and by reservation only. I want outdoor seating for the summer, and indoors I want it to feel like this restaurant. Not sure how a wine cellar would work out, but this sort of ambiance. It won't be a very big restaurant; it would seat thirty-five people inside max, so probably ten tables, which is why I think reservation only will work. I want an open kitchen where the tables can get a peek of the chef and cooks at work. I also want a fireplace that can be lit in the winter months, giving off the coziest warm glow for the customers."

Liz put her hands up to her mouth and smiled. "This sound incredible, Greg. I'm surprised you're just telling me."

Greg took a bite of the appetizer, savoring the softness of the cheese against the crustiness of the bread. "Well, it really all came together the other day. My friend Dale—who owns that restaurant Porridge in Collingswood—has a similar business model where it's only open three or four days a week and is reservation only, and he does phenomenally. He's offered to help mentor me. In fact, he said to stop by after here for some dessert on the house. We should have enough time to do that before seeing the property in Cape May."

Liz grabbed a bite of the appetizer, closed her eyes and smiled. "I can't wait."

After their scrumptious dinner, they drove to Porridge to take Dale up on his offer. Though they arrived to a packed house, Dale had set aside two stools along the seating area that faced the kitchen for them. They sat down, absorbing the energy and beauty of the small but vibrant place.

Dale was in the busy kitchen when he caught a glimpse of Greg and Liz.

"Hey, you two! Long time no see," Dale said as he leaned through the opening in the kitchen to shake hands with Greg and Liz.

Liz smiled. "This place is amazing, Dale. It looks like you're doing really well."

Dale grabbed a spoon and quickly tasted a big batch of carrot ginger soup that was offered by the cook. Nodding with approval to the cook, he looked back over at Liz and Greg. "Well, thank you. We are booked out for months. It's absolutely insane. I have offered to help mentor Greg while he figures out his plan."

Just then another cook handed him four desserts. Dale eyed the desserts and then added some final touches on each one—

white chocolate shavings and homemade caramel drizzle. When he was satisfied with their presentation, he handed them over to Liz and Greg.

"Here you go. These are our new desserts on the menu. Let me know how you like them. How about I get you two some cappuccinos to top them off," Dale said, then proceeded to call in the back for two capps.

Greg's eyes widened when he took a bite. "This is incredible, Dale. You are truly a master at this."

Liz rocked back and forth on her stool enjoying every single bite, when the artistic steaming-hot cappuccino was placed in front of her, it filled her nose with its full-roast aroma. She blew across the top a few times to cool it off before taking a slow, satisfying sip. She glanced around the restaurant and then back at Greg.

"The patrons here look so happy, as does the kitchen staff. Everything runs so smoothly. I don't think there's anyone better than Dale to show you the ropes. I'm excited," Liz said before taking another sip.

Greg smiled and put his arm around Liz. "I'm glad. We have to get going pretty soon to look at the property before it's dark out."

After they finished up and said their goodbyes to Dale and other staff members, they finally got on the road towards Cape May.

As they drove closer to the property, Liz realized how familiar the area was. "Wait, we're getting mighty close to home. Where exactly is this place?"

Greg laughed as he pulled into a parking spot on South Broadway Avenue in between bustling stores and other restaurants. "Well, we're here. Does it still look familiar?"

Liz gasped and put her hand over her mouth. "You're dad's old restaurant property? Are you kidding?"

Greg looked over at the place. It was a green Victorian house featuring a big front porch with ivy growing up the sides.

It stood elegant yet desolate and lonely among the other bustling shops and restaurants. While his father retained ownership of the property after closing his own restaurant, for years he'd rented it out to other entrepreneurs and businesses, but it hadn't been occupied for the past year while his dad had repairs done on it.

Greg laughed. "Well, believe it or not, my dad *finally* offered it to me after all of these years—and for a steal too. He had the roof repaired and a few other things taken care of, but I still have to do some remodeling inside, especially with the kitchen, which needs to be updated."

Liz jumped out of the car and hurried up the steps to the old place full of excitement. The sun had started to set and the lamppost nearby casted a warm glow onto the street and sidewalk.

Beside Liz, Greg unlocked the door and they walked inside the empty, creaky old house that had been converted into a restaurant. There were some random cobwebs and a window was slightly open somewhere, letting in the brisk February air.

Greg found and closed the window, then turned on some lights. "I mean, it doesn't look like much now, it's really just an unused house. But I have a major vision for it. The basement is completely unfinished, and I'd like to turn it into a wine cellar type eating atmosphere similar, but not nearly identical, to Bistro Fiorelli. I, of course, want to have my own take on it, and it will be BYOB, but will sell bottles of wine from small local wineries, which is allowed since we're selling on behalf of the winery."

Liz meandered around the space, admiring the cedar wood trim, while Greg talked. Her heart raced with excitement. "Didn't your dad say that there was a nice new patio out back?"

Greg smiled. "Yep, let's walk back there and take a look."

They walked out the back door into an adorable backyard,

though it was currently void of life and colors since it was winter.

Greg pointed to the brick patio area. "My dad thinks we could fit about five four-top tables out here. Then, on the front porch, about four or five more. It would be perfect for when the weather is nice. I envision lush, colorful flowers, a birdbath and fountain, and some cobalt-blue pots for decoration. I could really use your design help here, since you're the pro."

"Oh, you know I'm all over that. I'll have this restaurant looking shabby chic in no time. I think Margaret and Dave will have some good insight on what to plant in the backyard," Liz said, pulling out her phone. "I think Margaret should be on her way home right now. I'll see if she can swing by."

Liz rang Margaret, who immediately picked up. There was laughing in the background and Dave's voice. "Hey, Liz, what's up?"

Liz paced around the yard. "Are you with Dave?"

"Yes, I am. He's giving me a ride home since my car is having issues. What's going on?"

"Well, Greg and I have a little bit of surprise, and we want both of your input," Liz said excitedly.

Greg laughed, and spoke loud enough for Margaret to hear. "Yeah, you two. Swing by South Broadway. We're right next door to the burrito place."

"Wait, are you at his dad's property? The old restaurant?" Margaret asked.

"Yep. Greg's finally starting the process of opening a restaurant. Now get on over here," Liz said. After hanging up with her sister, she proceeded to sashay back into the house with Greg.

Margaret and Dave arrived five minutes later, pulling up out front and smiling at the sight of the place. It was in a perfect spot for a restaurant since the shops and other restaurants along the street already drew a big crowd.

Greg and Liz met them at the door and walked them

around the house, Greg going over the same things he'd told Liz about plans for the place.

Dave's eyes twinkled at the craftsmanship of the place. "Well, you know, after the film is over, I'll be available to help out with some projects."

"That would be awesome, Dave. Also, we wanted to get your input on the backyard. Follow me," Greg said as he made his way out to the back patio.

Margaret walked around the outside area, eyeing up the bushes, and snapping a twig off a low-hanging tree. "I'm picturing market lights strung above the tables, trimming this tree up, pulling out those overgrown bushes, and adding some colorful hydrangeas and perennials. I would also add some arborvitaes along the perimeter for privacy. They will make it feel much cozier here."

Liz and Greg smiled. "We knew you'd know exactly what to do with this area."

CHAPTER EIGHT

One early-March evening, Margaret and Liz pulled up for their evening shift at the B&B to countless cars in the driveway and on the street. Confused as they walked up the steps to the Seahorse, loud music blared from inside and lots of people could be seen milling about through the windows.

Liz pulled her key out of her pocket while pressing her face up to the glass window. "What on earth is going on? There're a ton of people here."

Margaret grabbed Liz's key from her hand but before she could even put it in the keyhole, Dolly flung the door open while Kim stood behind her.

"Margaret. Liz. So glad you're here," Dolly said with a nervous expression.

"Dolly, what's going on? Why are all these people here?" Margaret asked, peering inside.

Kim piped up. "We aren't exactly sure, to be honest. They started arriving a half hour ago, and they just kept piling in."

Dolly smiled and looked inside. "But did you see who these *people* are?"

Margaret and Liz walked into the foyer and looked around the bustling B&B. Suddenly, Liz's mouth dropped open.

"Is that *the* George Westwood?" Liz shrieked.

Margaret turned to look and threw her hand over her chest. "You've got to be kidding me. And he's sitting on our living room sofa. *Our* sofa."

Dolly and Kim nodded and smiled. "Keep looking. There's plenty more famous people you'll recognize around this place. I feel like we're hosting an awards party," Kim said with a chuckle.

Margaret glanced around the B&B and saw not one, not two, but twenty-five high-profile celebrities.

Just then, a young woman wearing a crisp long-sleeved black button-down shirt offered them a drink from the tray she carried. "Care for a glass of champagne?"

Margaret awkwardly grabbed a glass while Liz snatched one unabashedly and looked back at Dolly and Kim.

"Did you need us to stay? We are kind of enjoying being here, to be honest," Kim said as she stood gazing around, starry-eyed, at all of the celebrities.

Liz glanced at all of the food, plates, and glasses covering every flat surface of the B&B's furniture. "Well, it couldn't hurt to have extra help after everyone leaves."

Another woman circulated the room with a tray of plump, piping-hot soup dumplings.

Feeling like guests in their own establishment, the four ladies each grabbed a dumpling along with an appetizer plate.

Margaret popped the dumpling in her mouth and promptly screamed around it. "Oh my. It's hot. It's hot. The soup inside is searing my mouth. Grab me a napkin."

Katherine and William appeared with impeccable timing, walking down the staircase from the upstairs together. Katherine looked completely glam in her long-sleeved full-length body-hugging black velvet dress and fire-engine-red lipstick. Her long hair cascaded in soft luxurious red waves down the deep V of the dress's open back.

Katherine furrowed her brow as she saw Margaret eat the

soup dumpling the wrong way. "Margaret. You must bite the top of the dumpling first, then slurp the soup out before eating the rest. Otherwise, you'll burn your mouth."

Margaret made a half smile while fanning her mouth. "That would have been good to know thirty seconds ago."

Katherine laughed. "Why don't you two stay a while. Take your coats off. Enjoy the night. I've invited some friends over."

Liz's eyes widened. "*Some* friends?"

William grabbed Katherine's hand as she stepped off the stairs in her red stiletto heels. "Yes, I hope you don't mind. It was kind of last minute. I usually throw an Academy Awards after-party, but this year I wasn't able to, due to being here in Cape May shooting *Dinner under the Stars,* so I decided to bring the party to me." Katherine plucked a glass of champagne from the passing server.

William chuckled. "Katherine loves a good party. I hope you two don't mind."

"Margaret and Liz," Katie said as she and Erin descended the stairs. "So glad to see you two. Did you get my text messages?" Katie sounded little frazzled and looked a little disheveled.

Margaret and Liz both shook their heads. Margaret pulled her phone out of her pocket and saw an unread text from Katie thirty minutes ago, explaining the party. "I just did now."

"Well, I'm going to mingle. You all can stand here all night looking like sad lumps or you can follow my lead," Katherine said as she and William made their way into the living room.

Dolly and Kim made a beeline for the kitchen where one of their favorite childhood actors was sitting telling stories.

Erin and Katie pulled Margaret and Liz aside before they could go anywhere. "Sorry about the short notice, but we only found out about this thirty minutes ago ourselves, as well as Maria."

Liz squinted her eyes in confusion. "Who's cooking all of this food then?"

Maria appeared at the top of the stairs in a colorful ankle-length boho skirt and long-sleeved white cotton top adorned with dangling chunky necklaces. It fit her spunky, slightly-hippie personality perfectly. "Well, it ain't me. That's all I know. I'm going to savor this little break."

Erin looked Liz and Margaret up and down. "Are you two staying? Did you want to change into something a little *dressier* for the party?"

Liz looked down at the cable-knit sweater, jeans, and boots she had on. "Well, I guess we could pop back home and get changed …."

"Nonsense. Katherine's wardrobe takes up an entire room. She doesn't even know the half of what's in there. I'm sure I can find some things she wouldn't mind you two borrowing. Follow me," Erin said making her way back up the stairs.

Margaret and Liz vibrated with the giddiness of schoolgirls as they followed Erin and Katie to Katherine's "closet" while Maria also trailed after them to join in on the wardrobe selection.

One of the bedrooms had the bed pushed against the wall, and about ten clothing racks were filled to the brim with clothing that had never been worn yet. The room had a nice floral scent, which was probably from Katherine's many perfumes that lined the top of the dresser.

Erin bit her lip and walked over to a rack in the back, grabbing two different dresses, she handed one to Margaret and Liz. "Try these on and let me know what you think."

Since it was all women in the room, and it was one big closet after all, Margaret and Liz changed right there in the bedroom.

"Oh, I *love* it," squealed Liz as she looked at her own reflection in the floor-length mirror. As she spun around, the sequins of the short-sleeved body-hugging black dress sparkled under the light. "It shows off all the curves, but still hits just below the knee."

Margaret stared at herself in the mirror and gasped as Maria zipped up the back closure for her. The dress was a long off-the-shoulder gold gown with a front slit that came clear up to the outside of her right thigh. "I feel like a star."

Katie and Erin stood next to each other, smiles plastered on their faces, presumably proud of the one-minute makeover they'd conjured up. "Oh, I almost forgot. What shoe sizes are you?" Katie asked.

"Well, I'm an eight and Margaret is a nine," Liz said as she continued to stare into the mirror, having never seen herself in sequins before.

"Perfect. Katherine is a nine, and I'm an eight. We'll get you two some heels to go with them," Katie said as she marched out of the room.

After the shoes were retrieved, the heels added another few inches to their heights, and Margaret and Liz were ready.

"Wait! You're not quite done. Take your hair out of the ponytails. Let's put a little make up on you two. We'll throw a few curls in your hair and you'll be set."

Katie and Erin got to work quickly, not wanting to waste too much precious time away from the party. They were technically off the clock tonight, and wanted to take advantage of it.

"Just blot your lips on this tissue, and I think you two are done," Erin said as she stood back to study them as though they were her project.

"Holy cow. You two are beauts, if I do say so myself," Maria said as her tightly curled, long blonde locks danced around her head.

The sisters turned around to the mirror, each feeling a rush of happiness. Now that they felt wonderful, it was time to join the party.

"Before you go anywhere, let me spritz you," Maria said as she grabbed one of Katherine's many perfume bottles and began to spray the air in front of Margaret and Liz. "Step into the spritz and follow me. We're headed downstairs to rock this party."

Even if it was *their* B&B, and they were now elegantly dressed to fit the party, Margaret and Liz sure felt out of place. At least having Maria to follow around was something of a comfort. She was used to being around celebrities, after all.

Maria walked down the stairs with confidence, making her way into the kitchen as Margaret and Liz trailed behind. She hugged and kissed just about every one of the celebrities, all of them glad to see her.

Suddenly, she made an announcement to the room. "Hello, everyone. These are my friends, Margaret and Liz. They own this B&B," Maria said as she grabbed a dirty martini with blue cheese stuffed olives from the server's tray.

Margaret nervously smiled. Liz stiffly held up her hand to say hello.

George Westwood walked over to both of them. "Thank you, Margaret and Liz, for allowing this party of sorts at your B&B. Some of us flew in on our planes last minute for this."

Liz grabbed a few hors d'oeuvres from the server standing beside her. "Of course, George. So nice to meet you."

George smiled, casting his eyes upon Margaret. "You look stunning, if you don't mind me saying."

Margaret blushed, feeling slightly embarrassed by the attention. "Thank you. We just threw these outfits together pretty quickly."

Just then, Patricia Cramer, one of the most beautiful stars in Hollywood draped her arms around George's neck. "Come back to the living room, George. Vivian is telling her wonderful stories again."

George turned to her with a smile. "I'll be over in a minute."

Patricia walked away as he gazed back at Margaret, ignoring the fact that Liz was standing right next to her. "Well, I guess I'll talk to you later."

Once he was out of earshot, Liz turned to Margaret. "He's *totally* flirting with you."

Margaret, oblivious, grabbed one of the hors d'oeuvres from Liz's plate. "I don't think so. There are tons of beautiful celebrities here. Why would he flirt with *me?*"

Margaret looked towards the living room. Patricia was now draped across George's lap, talking to other celebrities in the room, but George had turned to glance back at Margaret.

"See what I mean," Liz said.

"Well, I have the perfect man already," Margaret said matter-of-factly. "Even *the* George Westwood couldn't sway my heart from Dave, even if it feels like I barely see him anymore since the film shoot has taken over our lives," Margaret said as she sighed and leaned her shoulder into the wall.

"Well, it looks like Katherine found the perfect man, too," Liz said as she motioned with her head to where Katherine and William canoodled by the stairs to the basement.

Margaret smiled. "I had a feeling that was what was going on."

Just then, Dottie Groff, another beautiful high-profile celebrity actor, sauntered over and stood next Margaret and Liz as they stared at Katherine and William.

"You see them? I think they had a little spark years ago, but nothing came of it. Then, they get cast in this movie here in Cape May together, and I think playing a couple onscreen made those feelings reemerge deeper than before. We all knew they were meant to be together. It's crazy how long it's taken for this romance to develop. Then again, the car accident didn't help matters."

Margaret nodded, not sure what to say. "Well, I'm glad to see they're happy," she finally said, turning to Dottie.

Dottie took a swig of her martini and glanced over at Patricia draped over George in the living room, who was telling stories about his days on Broadway before he got into films. "This is the happiest any of us have ever seen Katherine, you know. It could be her being here in Cape May. It could be her working again on something big, or it could be William. Maybe it's a mixture of the three."

Liz propped her elbow on the kitchen island. "Well, we've definitely seen a transformation in her since she first arrived."

Margaret scanned the room, her eyes landing back on George.

"And don't get me started on those two," Dottie said after following Margaret's gaze to George and Patricia. "I'm sure you read in the tabloids that they dated? Well, they've been broken up for a while now, but Patricia cannot seem to move on. He's just too nice of a guy about it. It's ruined a lot of his chances with other women, I'll tell you that," Dottie said as she pointed to herself.

* * *

It was a full, bright moon that night and Dave, Brad, Ricky, and the rest of the construction crew decided to try out a little night surfing. The waves were a lot smaller than they were used to in California, but that didn't matter. They craved time in the ocean.

Donning their wetsuits, they conjured some surfboards, and made their way to beach. They paddled out and waited for the ocean to cooperate, lining up next to each other on their boards, enjoying the soothing water, even if it was twenty degrees colder than the Pacific.

Dave looked over to see a seagull happily floating along next to him. "Hey, little guy. You enjoying this full moon too?"

The seagull looked at Dave as it bobbed in the water, not caring that they were a mere three feet from one another. Dave looked up at the moon, inhaling a deep breath of the salty air, and relished being in the water again. Suddenly a larger wave came up behind them.

Brad spoke up. "Dave, this one is all you. You've got it."

As the wave began to swell, Dave paddled furiously. When the timing was right, he planted his hands on the board, preparing to pop up, but before he could stand, he lost his balance, and plunged straight into the wave's frenetic energy. Dave was tossed and tumbled underwater, not knowing which way was up, until finally pounding his head into the sandy floor. The surfboard slammed against his leg, feeling like a million needles piercing his skin at the same time. The ocean spit him out to the beach where he lay writhing in pain. Everyone quickly paddled back to the beach to get Dave, who was holding his leg.

"I don't know, man. I don't think night surfing was probably the best idea for a dude who hasn't surfed in years," Ricky said to Brad.

Brad rolled his eyes at Ricky. "Dave, are you OK? Does it feel like something's broken?"

The rest of the crew had gotten to the beach and were surrounding Dave.

He paused and took a deep breath, rolling up the wet suit so the bottom part of his leg could be seen. His ankle was bright red and the size of a softball. "I think I did something nasty to my ankle."

Brad looked back at the rest of the group. "You all can get back out on the water. I'm going to take Dave to the ER to get this checked out. If it's broken, it needs to be taken care of right away."

Dave was able to stand and leaned on Brad as he hobbled back to the car. Once at the hospital, there was a little wait to be seen.

"I'm going to let Margaret know that I'm here," Dave said as he typed out a text on his phone.

After an hour, they were finally taken back. Dave told the nurse and doctor what happened, and the doctor took a look at his ankle. "Well, I'd like to get an X-ray of this so we can be sure it's not broken," he said as he pressed on the inflammation.

Once the X-ray had been completed, the doctor came back into the room. "Well, the good news is you didn't break it. The bad news is you did sprain it. I recommend resting, elevating it, and icing it to bring the swelling down."

With the lumbering use of crutches, Dave made his way out of the hospital with Brad walking slowly beside him. Just as they stepped out of the hospital's entrance, a black car with tinted windows pulled up in front of them. Margaret got out in a ball gown, heels in hand, and hurried over to Dave barefoot. "Are you OK? I just saw your text."

Dave's eyes twinkled as he appreciated how enchanting Margaret looked in her dress. "Well, I am now. It's just a sprained ankle. We did a little night surfing, and well, I'm not the young whippersnapper I used to be. I was way too rusty. We thought I broke it, there for a bit."

To his complete and utter shock, George Westwood stepped out of the same black car Margaret had just exited. Then, he walked right up to Margaret and put his arm around her back, pulling her in close. "Is everything OK here?"

Taken aback, Dave's focus zeroed in on his arm around Margaret. "Everything is just fine. Thanks, George," Dave said, perplexed and uncomfortable with the situation.

"Katherine is throwing a party at the Seahorse. They got Liz and I dressed up for the occasion. We just found out about all of it tonight when we arrived to work. I left my phone in my coat pocket, but I came as soon I saw your text message. George offered to have his driver take me when I told everyone why I was leaving."

George cleared his throat. "Yes, she's had some drinks, so it wasn't safe to drive. We can drive you home if you like," he said to Dave.

Dave bit his lip and looked over at Margaret. "I think I'm OK. Brad drove me, so I'll just go with him."

Margaret pulled away from the arm George still had postured around her and walked over to Dave. She hugged and kissed him, asking, "Are you sure? Is there anything I can do for you?"

Dave looked back over at George, feeling slightly defeated. "No, you go on and enjoy Katherine's party."

CHAPTER NINE

Early the next morning, Margaret and Liz were groggy when they arrived for their day at the B&B, having spent way too late of a night at the party.

Margaret yawned as she unlocked the front door. "I wonder where everyone went after the party last night?"

Liz rubbed her eyes and smoothed her shirt. "Who knows. It's looks like there are a few extra cars in the driveway still. Did you ever hear back from Dave after going to the hospital?"

Margaret shook her head. "Not since he left the hospital with Brad. He hasn't responded to my texts or called me back, which is not like him."

"That's weird," Liz said as she walked inside, nearly tripping over someone's yoga mat that was spread in front of the door. "Well, I don't think we have to wonder where everyone went."

"Now back into downward dog pose," Maria said from the living room.

About fifteen of the celebrities from the party the night before were sprawled across the foyer and living room doing a yoga class led by Maria. Candles had been lit and placed all over the first floor and calming meditation music played throughout. The shades were drawn and an aroma of lavender essential oil wafted in the air.

Katherine looked up from her pose at Margaret and Liz and motioned to the pile of yoga mats sitting in the corner.

Margaret glanced at Liz, who shrugged. Why not? she thought and followed her sister to grab a mat. The pair set them up near an open spot by the kitchen.

Maria was completely in her element. She had on tie-dyed harem pants, and her long blonde spiral curls were pulled high atop her head. It probably wasn't her first time conducting a class on the fly.

"Let's sink into child's pose," Maria said as the music slowed and softened.

The collective group of yogis let out a loud sigh, everyone finally letting their muscles relax.

"I'm going to walk around the room with eucalyptus oil now. If you'd like some on your wrist to breathe in, lay on your mat with your palms facing upwards," Maria said as she walked between the many mats around the rooms.

Margaret and Liz lay motionless on their mats. With a deep sense of calm, Liz closed her eyes and took deep breaths, letting each one sink her deeper and deeper into the mat.

"Hey, you two."

Margaret heard a familiar voice above her and opened her eyes. "Sarah?"

"I stopped over before heading to the coffeehouse to bring more of our roasted beans and some pastries, and Maria kind of convinced me to stay for yoga. My employees are opening Monarch Coffee this morning so it worked out. They need to learn to open without me there," Sarah said as she wiped sweat off of her forehead. "It's a good thing I keep workout clothes in the car."

Liz, not wanting to move from her relaxed state, smiled. "Well, thank you for bringing that over."

"I'm going to change and head out. I'll talk to you two

soon," Sarah said as she grabbed her stuff and quietly tiptoed out of the room.

Margaret closed her eyes again, when Maria placed a drop of eucalyptus oil on each wrist, she rubbed it in, placed it to her nose, and inhaled the woody, citrus smell that was both soothing and awakening at the same time.

After some deep meditation exercises, everyone eventually rolled up their mats and made their way back up to their rooms or other areas of the B&B.

Maria collected the candles, turned off the music, and walked into the kitchen. She immediately grabbed one of the Monarch Coffee bean bags Sarah had left on the kitchen island. Opening it, Maria inhaled deeply.

"This coffee is outstanding. She left it last time she was here and everyone loved it. I'm going to grind it up and brew some for everyone here," Maria said as she moved around the kitchen efficiently.

Margaret and Liz quickly freshened up then gathered two dozen mugs from the cabinet and arranged them on the table with creamers, sugars, and spoons.

Katherine walked in looking quite perfect for someone who'd just finished a sweaty workout. "How about that party last night, ladies? It was fabulous, wasn't it?"

Margaret looked over and smiled, having grown fond of Katherine.

"It was something. Did a lot of people spend the night?" Liz asked as she arranged a platter with the pastries Sarah had brought.

Katherine walked towards the kitchen window and looked outside. "Actually, yes. A lot of them did. If you're wondering where the gentlemen are, they're outside smoking cigars together."

Margaret and Liz walked to the window to see, and the first thing Margaret noticed was Patricia draped over William's lap.

He looked uncomfortable and awkward and not quite sure what to do about it.

Katherine noticed the scene at the same time. Her eyes squinted to get a better look, and then she turned away. "Well, that's enough of that."

Maria walked to the window and scoffed. "What is she doing on *his* lap? I've seen her sit on four guys' laps since the party. Does she flirt with everybody?"

Liz, loving that Maria said what everyone was thinking, nodded in agreement. She had surely seen it at the party too.

"Well, I'm going to my room. I'll be down later," Katherine said as she walked away stone-faced.

Maria walked back over to where the coffee was brewing and threw down a towel. "Katherine can't get a break. I'm over it. I was finally seeing the old Katherine here in Cape May. She's been happy again standing next to William. She was coming out of that shell that exudes fear, hurt, and anger … and now this. I won't allow it."

Maria opened the kitchen door and marched outside with angry curls bobbing furiously around her face. She didn't have a care in the world about who was a celebrity and who wasn't. She'd worked with them long enough to be completely impervious, they were no different than any other person.

"Patricia, get *off* of William. What are you trying to do? Katherine saw you, you know. How would you feel if you were in her shoes? And William … I know you're a nice man to a fault, but you can't allow this."

William immediately stood up. "You're right, Maria. This isn't appropriate, Patricia."

Patricia, possessing enough sensibility to at least look slightly embarrassed, walked over to George, who also sat among the group, and placed her hand on his shoulder. "I'm … sorry. I didn't realize."

George shook his head and took another puff of his cigar,

knowing full well she'd been unsuccessfully attempting to make him jealous with the whole ordeal.

William walked into the house and up the stairs towards Katherine's room.

Maria followed him back into the house but went into the kitchen.

As if nothing had happened, Maria piled her curls back atop her head, threw on a bandana, and turned up her music. Then she set about pouring coffee for everyone who had meandered into the kitchen.

* * *

When Judy and Bob walked into the modest old farmhouse they'd rented for the week in Tuscany, their eyes sparkled at its rustic beauty. It had two bedrooms, one for them and one for Ruth and Bill, and took a while to get to since it was off the beaten path, nestled among olive trees, farm animals, gardens, and vineyards.

Judy set her suitcase down inside the front door, and looked around the simple but darling place. It was quite chilly out so the owners had started a fire in the fireplace for them, and it crackled in the corner, warming the place nicely.

Walking over to the kitchen table, she found a couple of bottles of red wine with a welcome note.

Enjoy these wines made from grapes harvested on our vineyards.
Join us, along with other guests, for homemade
wood-fired pizzas at the Fratello building tonight.
Hope you enjoy your stay in beautiful Tuscany.

Just then, Ruth and Bill huffed and puffed their way over the threshold, suitcases in hand.

"How *much* did we pay for this shack?" Ruth snipped as she looked around at the many cracks along the walls and ceiling of the farmhouse. Judy didn't mind, she thought it gave the place character.

Bill shook his head at Ruth and grabbed her suitcase from her before hauling it down the hallway to their bedroom.

Bob chuckled. "Well, it's not a five-star hotel, but I think we'll get a unique experience staying here. It will be fun. Take a load off and relax."

Ruth furrowed her brow, then proceeded to shriek as a small bug ran right in front of her. "Bob! I can't do this. I feel like I'm renting out a barn."

Judy rolled her eyes, bit her tongue, and proceeded to their bedroom to unpack.

At dinnertime, the foursome walked across the way to the pizza gathering. The property was a working farm that took in volunteers and interns. Pizza night appeared to be something they did biweekly with guests, volunteers, and interns. It was a party of sorts.

The outdoor wood-fired oven had lots of people gathered around it. Adjacent to it stood a large table where people were talking and laughing while applying toppings to their pizzas before thrusting the pies into the oven. It was a mix of both local Italians and American guests.

Ruth eyed the pizzas and scrunched her nose. "Is that *pears* on the pizza?"

A woman chimed in, "Yep. This is one of the favorites here," she nodded down at the pizza she was creating. "It's pears, Gorgonzola, and caramelized onions with a balsamic drizzle. The sweet and savory pair so nicely together. You must try it."

Ruth laughed. "I think not. I'll stick to the plain pie. Is it like Domino's pizza? That's my favorite back home."

The woman laughed. "I would say that these are much better. A lot of these ingredients were grown here or at nearby farms. It doesn't get much fresher than this."

Ruth stuck her nose up to the sky and marched inside to

the long farmhouse dining table where other guests had already congregated with their pizza slices.

Judy glanced at Bob and rolled her eyes. "I'm not sure why Ruth came to Italy if she doesn't want to experience the amazing authentic food. Poor Bill, he has to do whatever she wants."

Bob shrugged and pulled out a seat for his wife. Just as Judy sat down and took a handful of olives from the bowl on the table, a scattering of items flew towards her in the air. Reflexively, she shielded her face.

"Here. I got a ton of these wet naps. We'll be needing them," Ruth said, chucking a few packets Bob's way.

Judy removed her arm from her face and looked down at twenty or so packages littered across the table. Some had landed in the olive bowls and on other guests' pizza plates.

"Uh, thanks?" Judy said as she quickly brushed all of them off the table and into her purse before further embarrassment overcame her.

After devouring many different pizza slices—both familiar flavors and unique combinations—they walked as a group on a sunset stroll to the ruins of a historic castle on the property.

Bob took Judy's hand in his and kissed it. Everything felt romantic and enchanting as they strolled the Italian countryside, enjoying the sunset after a wonderful meal.

Bill followed suit and grabbed Ruth's hand, except his reception didn't go as well.

"Hun, your hands are clammy," Ruth said as she pulled her hand away and stuck it in her pocket.

Bill shrugged it off, trying to not let it ruin the beautiful sunset.

As they walked uphill toward the top of the property, the sunset revealed itself more and more, and the castle ruins appeared directly in front of them. Their hosts turned on some celebratory Italian music and encouraged everyone to dance and enjoy themselves right there at the ruins.

Bob and Judy showed off their dance moves, the product of years of lessons, while Bill sheepishly looked over at Ruth, waiting to see what she would do.

Ruth breathed a deep sigh, realizing the uptight woman she'd become, took the pin out of her tight bun and let her shoulder-length gray hair down. Then she uncharacteristically threw her beloved and expensive purse into the dirt on the ground and held her hand out to Bob for a dance.

* * *

The next day, Sarah arrived to open up Monarch Coffee earlier than her employees. The sun had just started to rise over the ocean, and the street was quiet and peaceful as the morning glow crept in. She hadn't spoken to Mark in close to a couple of weeks, which was both crushing and liberating. She didn't want to settle for a relationship that wasn't fair to her and felt some time away from talking to one another was probably the best for both of them.

She walked inside, flicked on the lights, put her stuff down, and wrapped her apron around her waist. While preparing the coffee, she heard the front door open. Expecting it to be her employees, she didn't look up from what she was doing until she heard a familiar voice.

"Sarah?"

Sarah looked towards the door to see her neighbors from Cape Café down the street, Jen and Jon.

"Oh hi, you two," Sarah said, happy to have some company in the quiet place. Sometimes it hit her that she felt lonelier and lonelier the longer she didn't speak to Mark.

"Hey, Sarah. We thought we'd stop by and check out your place before starting work for the day at our cafe. How are things going?" Jen asked.

Sarah threw a towel over her shoulder, and leaned on the counter. "Oh, it's going. A little bit of a slow start. I thought it'd be a lot busier, but so far, it's mainly college kids coming in. You?"

Jen and Jon looked at each other, then grabbed seats at a table near the counter. "That's what we're worried about too. Our business has plummeted, and don't think for a second it's because of your business. As you remember, we told you it's been like this for months now. We're not sure how much longer we're going to be able to sustain like this."

Sarah walked out from behind the counter and plopped into a chair across the table from them. "You're kidding."

Jon shook his head. "We wish we were."

Jen looked out one of the tall windows towards the ocean. "We just don't get it. For so many years we did so well. We don't know what changed. Why did we start losing business?"

Sarah dropped her head back in the chair and looked up at the ceiling. "I don't know, but we've got to work together to change this."

Jon popped up out of his seat. "What if we threw a block party, got all the other stores on Beach Avenue to participate? It could be on the first day of spring, March 20. We'll offer special deals at our establishments, have food trucks, maybe get a band to play … that sort of thing."

A big smile grew on Sarah's face. "I like where you're going with this. It could work."

CHAPTER TEN

A week after Katherine's awards party, Margaret walked into the B&B and threw her bags down on a chair.

"Well, he hasn't spoken to me since the party," Margaret said out loud waiting for someone to hear her.

No one answered.

"Did anyone hear me? My boyfriend is not speaking to me!" Margaret said even louder this time.

Katherine, Dottie, George, and Vivian, plus a handful of other celebrities, yelled from the basement.

"Come down here and talk to us!" Katherine called.

Margaret, now desensitized to hanging out with celebrities, threw her head back in exasperation, and trudged down the steps into the basement Dave had so lovingly made into a home theater for her.

The room was dark and they had a classic old film on the screen, each person cozied up with hot freshly buttered popcorn.

"Now what's this you say? Dave isn't speaking to you?" Katherine asked, concern growing on her face.

Margaret slumped into one of the recliners and grabbed a

handful of popcorn right out of Vivian's bowl without asking. She stuffed some into her mouth and kicked her feet up. "Yes, that's right. He hasn't spoken to me since the night of the party."

"That's odd. Did something happen?" Vivian asked.

"No. George gave me a ride to the hospital that night when I went to meet him after his surfing accident. He acted weird and then hasn't returned my calls since," Margaret said, stuffing another handful of popcorn into her mouth.

George cleared his throat. "Was he mad that I was in the car with you?"

Margaret sighed, staring up at the starry ceiling. "No, he's not one to get jealous. Ever. Plus, all you did was give me a ride. What is there to be mad about?"

George, oblivious, shrugged. "Beats me."

Maria, having overheard the conversation from upstairs, marched down the red-carpeted steps into the basement. "Margaret, you need to tell him how you feel. Promise me you will not let that amazing man get away."

Margaret let out an aggravated sigh and grabbed another handful of popcorn, this time chasing it down with Vivian's soda. "How exactly can I do that if he won't return my calls?"

Maria propped a hand on her hip and tossed her blonde curls back. "Duh. You go find him."

Margaret, finally registering the extra celebrities from the party were still at the B&B, sat up in her chair. "So, am I missing something? Is everyone here visiting you, Katherine?"

Katherine laughed. "Well, I was wondering when you would notice."

Margaret furrowed her brow in confusion.

"One of the producers at the party asked a bunch of them to stay and do cameos in the film. They're all staying here with me. I hope that's OK."

"Yes, of course. The more the merrier."

Margaret jumped out of her chair, still feeling heartbroken, and walked to the table with the candy. She grabbed a chocolate bar and felt a familiar touch. George was beside her, his hand on her back, just like he'd done when she went to meet Dave at the hospital.

"Sorry, dear. Just need to grab my bag beside you," George said as he reached underneath the table.

A lightning bolt thought struck her hard. George had had his hand on Margaret when she met Dave at the hospital. Had Dave thought something was going on?

* * *

The next day on the film set, Dave hobbled around, helping to put finishing touches on a room in Katherine's character's house for an upcoming scene that was scheduled for the following day.

Brad grabbed some boards and nailed them up to close up a hole. "You OK, man? You've been pretty quiet lately."

Dave looked over. "Who, me? Oh, yeah, I guess. I'm OK."

Brad stopped what he was doing, looked back over at Dave, and cocked his head to the side. "I don't believe that for a second. What's going on?"

Dave pulled a nail out from his tool belt and with one fell swoop, smashed the nail straight into the board with his hammer. "Well, actually, I've been kind of in the dumps since that ... night."

"The surfing accident last week? Oh, man. I'm so sorry. I feel horrible. It was your first time surfing in years, and it was my bright idea to go at night," Brad said shaking his head.

Dave scratched the back of his neck and pulled off his backwards hat, running his hands through his hair. "No, it wasn't that. It's just ... Margaret arrived with George Westwood to come see me."

Brad chuckled. "Yeah, I noticed. So, she hangs with those celebrities? I'm only used to working with them."

Dave sighed. "I guess she does now. I had no idea. Then, he walked up behind her and put his hand on the small of her back when she was talking to us at the hospital. It shook me up."

Brad furrowed his brow. "Why? I don't think it meant anything."

Dave slammed another nail into a board with a hammer, this time with more force than necessary. "Well, it's where I put my hand on her. And it's where I saw my ex-best friend's hand on my ex-wife's body when I caught them cheating on me. That little gesture … it destroyed me right in that moment."

Brad threw his arms over his head. "Oh, my man. I'm so sorry. Why didn't you say something?"

Dave shook his head and powered another nail into the board. "I couldn't. I'm the boyfriend who never gets jealous. I'm perfect in her eyes. I didn't want to screw it up with my past trauma."

Irene, overhearing the conversation, walked up onto the set.

"Hey, you," Irene said to Brad in a flirty voice as she gently touched his arm.

Brad's cheeks turned a bright shade of red, and a wide smile appeared on his face. "Hey, Irene. How's it going?"

Irene walked over to Dave. "Everything is going OK, but what's this I hear you guys talking about? What's your past trauma going to screw up?"

Before Dave could answer, Irene hit her walkie button, talking into her headset. "Copy that. Katherine is on set. The construction crew is just about done."

Dave hit another nail into the board. "Just my past trying to ruin my current, amazing relationship with Margaret."

Katherine appeared on set, half reciting her lines but

staring at Dave. "What about your relationship with Margaret?"

The assistant director walked into the room. "OK, everyone off the set. We've got a scene to shoot."

Katherine held up her hand. "Give me five minutes, please."

The assistant director sighed and walked over to craft service to make his tenth cup of coffee for the day.

Dave, suddenly feeling embarrassed, walked over to Katherine. "I'm just unsure of everything right now."

Katherine stared at Dave for a moment before saying point-blank, "Well, you need to start making yourself sure of things. I know for a fact that Margaret cares for you."

Dave swallowed hard. "I care for her too. I just don't know if my past is going to ruin things between us. I saw George's hand on her when she came to see me at the hospital and all this pain and hurt came rushing back, just like when I discovered my ex-wife cheating on me."

Katherine laughed. "George's hand? On Margaret? That's what this is about? He does that to everyone."

Dave breathed a sigh of relief. "I haven't talked to her in a week. Have I ruined everything?"

Katherine glanced over at William as he stood off to the side of the set reciting lines for the scene. Aside from doing their scenes together, they had also barely spoken since the morning after the party when Patricia was draped on him. It had all been very awkward; she may have had to take her own advice.

Katherine looked back over at Dave. "No, you haven't ruined anything. Now go get our girl."

The assistant director finished his coffee and looked at his watch. "Alright, clear the set for real this time. We've got a scene to shoot."

Dave looked at Katherine with a smile on his face as anxiousness built inside of him.

* * *

Greg flicked the lights on in the restaurant, leaned against the wall, and gazed at the work that had already been done. It had been a a few weeks already and the kitchen had been gutted, awaiting it's remodel and new appliances. He'd hoped it would be able to open just in time for the start of the summer rush.

Liz walked in, slowly shutting the door behind her and pulling off her jacket. "It's unseasonably warm right now. I know the first day of spring is approaching, but I'm not used to this."

Dave laughed. "Take a look out back. Spring is sure rearing its head out there."

Liz was met with a flurry of purple and yellow crocuses along the brick patio. Behind them were hyacinths, tulips, and daffodils pushing through the soil. Birds happily chirped their songs as the sun peeked its head out from behind a cloud, casting warm rays upon her. What really captured her attention were the giant pergolas, cobalt-blue planted pots lining the yard, and the white market lights strung high above the patio.

Greg stood on the back porch overlooking the yard. "It's beautiful, isn't it?"

Liz smiled. "Let me guess. Did Margaret do this?"

Greg flicked the market lights on, and also activated a water fountain birdbath on the other side of the yard. "I'm pretty sure it was her, though she never told me she did it."

Liz sat down on the brick patio, closed her eyes, and let the sun warm her body all the way through. "I'm envisioning great conversations and food out here. People will make lasting memories over wonderful meals."

Greg sat next to her. "Oh yeah? What else do you envision?"

Liz closed her eyes again and took a deep breath. Greg did the same. While Liz was trying to relax and manifest the future, Greg was struck by visions of himself as a little boy at his father's restaurant—the same building he'd be opening his own restaurant in. His memory recalled it being dusk, and he saw himself as a boy, about nine years old, running down the long wide sidewalk out front. He stopped three feet short of the steps up to the building, taking notice of his father standing out back in the very yard where he now sat. His father was with someone. His mother? No, this woman looked much younger. They embraced and kissed. Greg squinted his eyes to get a better look, too young to really understand what was happening, but old enough to know that woman should not have been kissing him.

Greg cringed. "Ugh!"

Startled, Liz's eyes abruptly opened. "What's wrong?"

Lying down on his back, Greg put his arms behind his head and stared up at the clouds in the sky. "Oh, memories started to flood my head of this place, and not all of them are good ones."

"What do you mean?"

Greg sighed, but continued staring at the clouds. "Well, I've never told anyone about this, and frankly I've pushed it out of my brain since it happened, but when I was around nine, I saw my dad kissing another woman right where we're sitting."

Liz's mouth dropped open. "What? Are you serious? Who was it?"

"I'm pretty sure it was the young pretty hostess of the restaurant."

"I'm so sorry you had to see that. That must have been hard for nine-year-old boy. What did you do?"

"I did nothing. I didn't want my parents to divorce. I just hoped that my dad would come to his senses, and he must have. They're still together, and happy to boot, but it still eats me up sometimes when I have flashbacks," Greg said, turning to look Liz square in the eyes.

Liz felt her heart drop in her chest. "I'm so sorry that

you're reliving that awful moment. You've never brought it up to your father?"

Greg shook his head. "I don't have to. He saw me. He knew I saw everything and maybe that was a good thing. Maybe he knew he couldn't sneak around anymore if he wanted to keep his family together."

Liz closed her eyes and rested her head on Greg's chest. "I have to confess something. When I asked for a divorce last year, it was partly because I'd connected with another man."

Greg sat up, pulling away from Liz's arms. "What? Who?"

Liz stood up. "Now before you freak out, just know that nothing happened."

Greg stood up next to her. "OK, but who?"

"It was Todd, my high school boyfriend."

Greg scoffed. "You're kidding. You're just now telling me this?"

Liz stared at her feet. "I was unhappy with our living situation. I wanted to be closer to my family and the beach in Cape May. I was unhappy with us, and we weren't connecting like we used to. I was out with friends when I ran into him. We talked all night. That was it. That's all that happened. But when I asked for a divorce after that night, you changed. We changed. We started working together to make each other happier, and now we have this gorgeous home in Cape May and you're opening your dream restaurant."

Greg, still feeling a little upset, took a deep breath and blew it out. "So, you never had an affair?"

Liz smiled and walked to her husband, wrapping her arms around him. "No, not even close. Frankly, I'm not sure we'd be as happy as we are now if I hadn't asked for that divorce."

Greg kicked a small rock by his foot and pulled Liz in closer to him. "I don't ever want to lose you."

Liz kissed Greg and leaned her head against his chest, deep in thought. "Do you think both of us having these new, demanding businesses will be too much for our little family?

Will we have enough time for the kids? Will our love for each other hold strong?"

Greg nuzzled his face into Liz's hair and kissed her head. "I think we'll figure it out. It may not be easy at first, but I know we'll always prioritize our family."

CHAPTER ELEVEN

Spring would be springing at the end of the week with March 20 only a few days away, and it was quite an eventful time in Cape May. The film shoot was wrapping up and The First Annual Beach Avenue Block Party rapidly approached.

Margaret arrived to the B&B still feeling unsettled about her relationship with Dave. They had been playing phone tag, and kept missing the chance to really sit down and talk to one another. The movie in town didn't help any with that, keeping them both very busy on two different sides of it, her with Katherine at the B&B and him with the construction crew on set. Aside from some small chitchat text messages, nothing had been resolved between them.

Maria chatted with someone in the kitchen as Margaret walked inside. It was an unseasonably warm week in March with temperatures in the mid-seventies, which gave everyone a little more pep in their step. When Margaret walked into the kitchen, she discovered Sarah was the one talking to Maria.

"Hey, Margaret," Sarah and Maria said in unison.

"Hey, you two. What's going on?"

Sarah slumped back down into her seat, leaning her head on her arm. "I was waiting for you to get here and told Maria about our attempt to revive the businesses with the Beach Avenue block party in a couple of days."

Margaret furrowed her brow. "A block party?"

Sarah looked over at Margaret with confusion. "Yeah. Didn't I tell you?"

Margaret sat down next to her. "Nope."

Sarah sighed. "I'm so sorry. I thought I told you. My mind has been bogged down with so much lately. Since business is slow for myself and some of my neighboring stores, including Cape Cafe, we're hoping to drum up business with a block party. It could be a win-win for everyone."

Margaret smiled. "That's great. It sounds like you're all pulling together. I love that."

Sarah looked down at her hands. "Yeah, I just hope it works."

Maria poured some freshly brewed Monarch coffee into some mugs for the three of them. "Well, I'll tell you what. Your coffee is some of the best I've ever had, and I've been just about everywhere while working as a personal chef for celebrities."

Just then, Katherine arrived with a group of her friends followed by Katie and Erin.

"Oh, is that *the* coffee? I need a cup. We all need a cup. It's exquisite," Katherine said as she hovered near the coffee pot.

Maria poured their mugs while Sarah laid out boxes of pastries. "The coffee and these pastries are from my new coffeehouse, and these pastries are from Cape Cafe, the vegan coffee place near me. Business is quite slow, unfortunately. Hopefully, the block party this week helps remedy that."

Vivian grabbed a chocolate almond croissant and washed it down with a sip of hot coffee. "This is some of the best I've ever had. How on earth is business slow?"

Sarah smiled and shrugged. "I'm not sure exactly."

Katherine grabbed one of the vegan scones and took a gulp of the coffee. "This is outstanding. And it's vegan? It's so hard to find good vegan pastries these days. I wish there was a way we could help."

A light bulb went off in Katie's head, and she pulled out her clipboard and began feverishly writing. After she was done, she ripped off the piece of paper and slammed it down on the kitchen island in front of everyone.

"There's my idea. I think it just might work," Katie said feeling quite proud of herself.

Everyone gathered around the piece of paper to read it. Sarah was the last to take a look. "Wow. You all would do that?"

Everyone nodded in agreement.

A knock came at the door, and Margaret answered to find Irene standing there with her headset on, papers in hand. "Hey, Margaret. I just needed to drop off this call sheet for Katherine for the last shoot day. I can't believe it's almost over."

Margaret smiled and hugged her. "Come on in, we're all talking in the kitchen."

"Sounds good. I have a few minutes," Irene said following her into the kitchen.

Katherine smiled and walked towards Irene. "It's Irene! Do you all know how hard she's been working on this film? She's in charge of wrangling me, and that's no easy feat. This girl deserves an award."

Irene blushed and gratefully accepted the hot mug of coffee that Maria placed in her hands.

"While I have you all here, I need a big favor," Katherine said, turning serious before looking at everyone in the room one by one. "As you know, William and I have fallen in love, but since the awards party, things haven't been the same.

"I have a very emotional last scene with him this week, and I was ready to back out of it. I knew I wouldn't be able to handle it. That's where my favor comes in. Normally, most actors and directors want everyone off the set for those types of scenes, but I want you all there. I need support. That includes *all* of you. I will make sure the director and assistant director are aware of this."

"Of course, we'll be there," Vivian said as she pulled her in for a big hug.

Margaret, Liz, and Sarah all nodded. "We'll definitely be there for you," Margaret said.

* * *

Judy and Bob boarded the plane that would take them back home. Although they had planned to visit other parts of Europe, they'd fallen in love with Italy and hadn't been able to tear themselves away. The same could not be said for Ruth, and thank goodness her and Bill had a separate flight home.

Having settled in their seats, the couple buckled up and prepared for takeoff. Judy laid her head on Bob's shoulder and squeezed his hand. Taking off was her least favorite part of the flight.

"It was a wonderful trip, Judy," Bob said as he clasped her hand and looked out the window of the plane.

Judy sighed. "It was and I can't wait to do it again, but I think I need a vacation from our vacation. I've never walked that much in my life. It's quite different than those vacations where you just sit on the beach reading and listening to the ocean waves. Speaking of which, I'm so excited to get back home to our beach town and see everyone."

Bob nodded. "I loved this vacation, but I can't wait to get back to our home sweet home. There really is no place like home."

"I'm going to miss our daily adventures in Italy. Maybe we can take little adventure road trips," Judy said looking at Bob with a big grin on her face.

Bob smiled. "Maybe you'll be able to meet Katherine Duffield."

Judy laughed. "We'll see."

* * *

Greg's restaurant was coming along nicely, and the planned summer open date seemed more achievable. Liz thought long and hard about their deep conversation on the brick patio behind the restaurant and had decided to make some changes.

It was Greg's forty-seventh birthday, and he hadn't wanted to do anything but work on the restaurant due to pure excitement. Liz got a babysitter, put on her finest little black dress, bought takeout from a nearby restaurant, and quietly set up a candle-lit table outside on the patio while Greg ran an errand for the restaurant.

About thirty minutes later, the dinner was ready, and Liz awaited her husband's return as the sun began to set. Greg walked up the sidewalk to the restaurant, bags in hand, and stopped right before the steps, in the exact spot where he'd watched his dad with the hostess. Something caught his eye in the backyard, and his stomach dropped. In a flash, the feeling morphed into a flutter when he saw his gorgeous wife waiting for him.

Greg walked to the backyard with a big smile on his face. Placing the bags on the ground, he scooped Liz up for an enormous hug and kiss, almost exactly where his dad had stood. "What is all this?"

Liz kept her arms around him and looked over at the table. I got us some takeout from your favorite Thai restaurant and set up a birthday dinner for us while you ran an errand. I couldn't let your birthday get away without doing a little something."

Greg laughed. "Well, this is spectacular. Let me bring these bags inside, and I'll be right out."

Liz nodded, tucked her dress underneath her, sat down in the chair, and poured a glass of wine.

Minutes later, the patio lights flicked on, then dimmed, and some Grateful Dead sounded through the outdoor speakers, one of Greg's favorite bands of all time.

Greg stepped outside looking a little more dapper, having dragged a comb through his hair and tucked his shirt in.

Liz's plan unfolded as planned. Along with celebrating Greg's birthday, she'd wanted to form a new, happier memory on that patio for him, and so far, it worked perfectly.

* * *

Sarah tied her ponytail up in a red ribbon and smoothed her black-and-white gingham apron while preparing Monarch Coffee for another day of business, or lack thereof. The First Annual Beach Avenue Block Party was tomorrow and some slight optimism had crept up inside of her. She had worked with Jon and Jen and a few other businesses to prepare for their big event, and she was hopeful they'd garnered enough attention and had spread the word well enough, but there would be no telling until the day of.

A handsomely rugged bearded man with a ratty trucker hat entered the shop just as some other employees got there. Wearing a plaid shirt, jeans, and boots, he walked up to the counter with a wide grin on his face. He had a saltwater smell about him and the most perfectly straight, white teeth Sarah had ever seen on such a rugged-looking man.

"Hey, there. I've been meaning to come in since you opened. I'm Chris. I run the Blue Heron Birding Boat down the street." He extended his hand while eyeing the place up and down.

Sarah smiled and shook his hand. "I'm Sarah, the owner. I didn't even know we had a birding boat here in Cape May. Sounds intriguing."

Chris laughed. "Oh, yeah. I get birders from all over. Cape

May is a great place to see the wildlife. My sunset tours are pretty popular. You'll have to come check it out sometime."

"Sounds good. What can I get you, Chris?" Sarah said feeling a little more chipper.

"Hmm … let's see. I'll have a black coffee."

Sarah walked over to grab a to-go cup. "Are you sure you don't want to try something a little fancy? Our lattes are pretty popular. I can even do a fun design on the top with the foam," Sarah said with a giggle.

Chris smiled and stared over at Sarah with a little twinkle in his eye. "Maybe next time. So, Sarah, how is business so far?"

Sarah poured his coffee and set it in front of him. "It's slower than I'd like, and other businesses on this street are suffering, as well. But I love the location and the work itself. Some of the other store owners and I actually planned a block party tomorrow here on Beach Avenue to help bring more people out this way. Have you heard about it?"

Chris scrunched his brow. "That's strange. I have not. Did you advertise? I usually keep up-to-date with events going on around here."

Sarah thought for a moment. "Well, there was a write-up in the local paper about it, and we passed out some flyers. I think Jon and Jen, the owners of Cape Café, did some things on social media as well, but I'm not sure."

Chris took a sip from his cup. "Wow. This coffee is outstanding. This may be my new go-to spot in the mornings before I get the boat ready for the day. What time is the block party tomorrow? Maybe I'll bring my son over. Will there be anything for an eight-year-old to do?"

Sarah leaned forward on the counter and cupped her chin in her hands. "Well, I happen to know there will be a Ferris wheel and a bounce house and some pretty cool food trucks. I hear funnel cake is involved. There will also be games, music, and my wonderful coffee and pastries, among other things," Sarah said with a wink.

Chris sipped from his cup again and closed his eyes as he took in the moment. "Well, that sounds like it's right up his alley. Maybe we'll see you there."

Sarah smiled and looked over to greet her two employees who had walked up to the counter while putting on their aprons. "Yes, most definitely. Just look for the gal with the bow on her ponytail."

Chris reached his hand out to Sarah, lingering as she shook it again. "Well, it was really nice meeting you, Sarah."

"It was nice meeting you as well. Enjoy the beautiful weather this week," Sarah said, feeling her heart flutter slightly as their hands were still clasped together.

Chris smiled, let go of Sarah's hand, and walked out of the coffeehouse. Meanwhile, Sarah's two employees immediately laughed and rolled their eyes.

"What?" Sarah asked confused.

April put her hand on her hip. "Oh, please. It was plain as day that he was flirting with you."

Doug stood behind April and snapped his fingers in the air. "Girl, he was fine. Get your broken heart over that Mark guy and move on."

Sarah smiled, feeling her heart flutter again, but then groaned and threw her head into her hands. "Ugh. Why is love so hard? This is why I have been single for so long."

April patted Sarah's back. "It's just how it is. I've had my share of broken hearts. In the end, they don't seem to matter when you finally find that right person, though. Are you and Mark getting back together when he gets home?"

Sarah stood up. "I don't think so. I mean, I don't know … I didn't spend most of my entire adult life single only to end up with someone who still makes me feel single since they're never here and always traveling for work."

Doug walked back to the conversation at the counter after

grabbing something from the back. "Puh-lease tell me you aren't hemming and hawing over what to do about Mark? Girl, we saw how miserable you were when he left. Get on out there in the world and date. See what there is to offer … and start with Chris," Doug said nudging April with a giggle.

Sarah walked over to make herself a cup of coffee. "Fine. Maybe I will."

CHAPTER TWELVE

For the final scene of the movie, just as Katherine had asked, her full entourage was present for moral support, including Margaret and Liz. The director and assistant director looked befuddled by all of the people standing around on set, but shrugged their shoulders and just went along with it. If it meant they could finish the scene in a timely manner without too many takes, then so be it. Everyone on the crew was tired —exhausted, really—from working twelve-plus-hour days. They were ready to be finished, and this last scene was the end of the film shoot in Cape May.

William stood in the corner of the room getting touched up with makeup while reciting his lines and nervously glancing over at Katherine. Katherine paced the other side of the room, reciting her lines and staring at the floor. She wanted this scene to be everything it needed to be. Ironically, she was living the scene on and off camera. Not much had to be acted, actually. In the film, William and Katherine played lovers who'd had a falling out and this scene was the rekindling of their romance.

"Irene, we need Katherine and William on the set now," the assistant director said into the walkie.

"Copy," Irene said, heading over to Katherine.

Within minutes, Katherine and William stood on the set together trying to tune into their characters.

The director gave them a little pep talk about the scene and walked back to his monitor behind the camera.

"Rolling. Quiet on the set," the assistant director said.

Katherine took a deep breath and immediately became Diane. "Did you always love her when we were together? Was it always her you thought about when we kissed? Am I nothing to you?" Tears streamed down her face.

"No, it was never her. It was always you. Always. Can't you see that?" William said as Tom.

"See what? Her lips on yours? Yes, I saw that plain as day. I certainly didn't see anything else," Diane said, slamming her fist against the wall out of frustration.

Tom sat at a desk and placed his hands over his face. "She kissed me. I never kissed her in return. I was taken aback by the whole thing. You saw the split second when it happened, but didn't stay to see me tell her to stop. You ran off and wouldn't speak to me for weeks."

Diane wiped a tear off her eye with a sleeve and walked to the window, looking out. "Well, what do you we now?"

Tom pulled his hand off his face to reveal watery eyes. "I guess we start over. We start right from the beginning as brand-new lovers. We fall in love again."

Diane ran to him, nestling her face into his shoulder, sobbing, while Tom wrapped her up in the tightest hug.

The set was completely silent. Not a breath could be heard.

Tom fiddled with something in his pocket and proceeded to get down on one knee. "I know I'm not perfect. I know we're not always perfect together, but I want to grow old with you. I want to cuddle by the fire on Christmas together. I want to eat out at our favorite restaurants together. I want to wake up next to you forever. Will you be my wife, Katherine?"

"Cut! Cut," the director yelled as he walked towards set

again. "That was perfect but you said *Katherine* instead of *Diane*. Let's start that over. OK, quiet on the set … and … action."

William still knelt with the ring, staring at Katherine. "I am asking you to marry me, here in front of everyone. There is nothing more in this world that I want but to have you by my side through life. I'm in love with everything about you, and I don't want to lose you, Katherine."

Katherine stood with her mouth agape, slowly pulling herself out of character. "What are you doing? We have to start the scene over, remember?"

William smiled. "I'm not acting, Katherine. This is my ring and the prop ring is in the other pocket. This is real. This is William talking to Katherine. Will you marry me?"

The crew, now realizing what was going on, stood in quiet anticipation of what was to come next. Katherine's entourage, on the other hand, jumped up and down, high fiving, unable to contain their squeals of excitement.

Katherine wiped real tears from her eyes this time and extended her hand to William. William placed the beautiful, huge diamond ring on her finger, then stood up as Katherine embraced and kissed him.

The director cheered. "Was that a yes, Katherine?"

Katherine walked out to the edge of the set, with the sparkling diamond ring, facing everyone. "Yes! I said *yes!* We're getting married!"

The set erupted in cheers. Catering happened to have some bottles of champagne on hand, having planned to celebrate the final scene. They quickly brought them out since the happy couple gave the crew and their friends something unexpected to rejoice in.

Katherine walked back over to William for a long kiss, looked back over at her entourage and gave a thumbs-up, then looked back over at the director. "Alright, let's get this scene right this time. We all want to go celebrate at this wrap party tonight, right? Plus, I've got a little something to do today for someone important."

* * *

Sarah buzzed around, prepping her coffee tent setup outside for the Beach Avenue block party happening that afternoon. The weather was a perfect sunny March day, and all had gone according to plan.

Jon and Jen had set up their tent in front of Cape Cafe before walking over to Sarah. "We really hope this helps draw attention and customers to our businesses. It really does feel like a last-ditch effort," Jen said as she helped Sarah put out her coffee cups.

"I do, too, guys. If nothing else, it will be a fun, beautiful day spent outside," Sarah said optimistically.

The block party had been scheduled to start at noon and run until five. Many food trucks lined the streets and the other businesses had set out their own displays of items for sale in front of their stores as well. A small stage stood right in front of the beach, and a DJ played Top 100 hits from the two speakers on either side of the stage.

Right around noon, people started appearing along the street, and by one o'clock, there was some hustle and bustle but not nearly as many people as they'd hoped for.

Moments later, black luxury cars pulled up to the stage, and a slew of people got out. Sarah craned her neck to see what was going on.

Katherine emerged from the crowd and walked onto the stage, grabbing the microphone. "Check, check. OK, good. We've got sound. Hi, everyone! So glad you could make it. I'm Katherine Duffield. You may have seen me in some movies. We've got a little surprise for you today."

People who'd been walking around the block party stopped in their tracks to stare at the stage in amazement. In a flurry, the crowd began taking photos, no doubt posting them immediately on social media. Some called or texted friends, stunned by what was going on.

Katherine pointed to the group of people that had arrived with her and motioned for someone to come up and join her. Then, one of the biggest pop singers in the world jumped on stage.

"Hey, everyone! I'm Joey Dinatto. We haven't done a single sound check, and I don't have my normal sound guys or equipment here, so you'll have to bear with me for this set, but we're going to do it. I do need a little help, though." He motioned back to the crowd of people who'd emerged from the black cars to come up on stage.

Katherine stood smiling as Vivian, William, Dottie, George and the rest of the celebrity gang lined up in a row behind Joey, waiting for whatever came next. Good thing they weren't a shy bunch.

By now, the crowd of spectators had nearly tripled and grew by the minute.

Joey pointed to the DJ, who was shocked but delighted. "Hey, buddy. Do you have any of my tracks from my newest album on your list?" The DJ nodded. "Mind playing them?"

The DJ smiled as his fingers flew across his laptop's keyboard, pulling up a karaoke music track without the vocals.

When the music started, Joey sang and his celebrity backup dancers did some hilarious, improvised choreography, which the crowd loved.

The throng of people grew bigger and bigger, and tons of folks were going in and out of the shops, eating from the food trucks, riding the Ferris wheel, and buying from the shop tents.

After an hour-long set of music, Joey performed one last song, this time asking the DJ to cut the music. He brought his acoustic guitar up, positioned one microphone in front of it and arranged another on a stand in front of his mouth. With the opening chords of his number one current hit, "To Be

With You," the celebrities onstage partnered up to slow dance, William and Katherine in the forefront.

Sarah, giddy with excitement, let her employees take over the tent in order to walk over to Jon and Jen's booth. She was thrilled to see a line down the block of customers waiting to buy something from them.

Jen stopped what she was doing and ran into Sarah's arms. "This is seriously the best day ever! I can't believe this. I haven't had a second to stop and enjoy the music or watch the stage. Can you believe we have celebrities at our block party? Do you see this line that we have?"

Sarah squealed. "My shop just sold out of our bagged roasted coffee beans and there's a long line of people too. I can't believe this!"

Joey finished his song, thanked the crowd, then jumped offstage, greeting the fans to give autographs and take pictures.

Katherine grabbed the microphone as the crowd screamed and cheered. "OK, give it up for Joey! Isn't he great?"

The crowd roared again, and Katherine looked down the street to see hundreds, if not thousands of people walking, shopping, and enjoying themselves. "Before we go, I want to take a minute to shout-out a few of my favorite places right here in Cape May. Monarch Coffee is outstanding, and I suggest you all check it out. We absolutely love their coffee. And Cape Café has amazing pastries. I've fallen in love with their specialty vegan lattes and scones and want everyone to go check them out."

Jon looked astonished and Jen threw her hand over her mouth, stunned that a celebrity was endorsing their little coffee establishment. Meanwhile, Sarah jumped up and down, waving at the stage. When she caught Katherine's eye, she blew her a kiss.

"Do you know her?" Jen said with pure shock.

Sarah laughed. "You can say that."

Jen giggled. "You might want to turn around. I think someone wants to talk to you."

Sarah spun around with a smile on her face to see Chris standing with his son.

"Well, I was wondering if we'd run into you. This is my son Sam. Sam, this is Sarah. She is running this fun event and owns that coffeehouse we just stopped at."

Sam put his hand out for a handshake and looked over at the bounce house. "Cool, can I go on the bounce house now?"

Chris laughed. "Go ahead. I'll watch from here."

Sarah smiled, recalling what her employees had said about Chris the other day. "Are you guys having fun? Did you see who was on the stage?"

"Oh, that Joey guy. My son loves him, but he's not so much my type of music. I saw Katherine Duffield gave you a shout out as we were walking. *That* was seriously awesome," Chris said, smiling from ear to ear.

Jen had gone back to helping Jon, so Sarah and Chris stood together as the multitudes of people passed them by.

Chris rubbed his neck and imposed a lingering look on Sarah. "So, do you have plans tomorrow? I was just thinking …"

Sarah took her apron off, revealing a cute retro floral-print dress paired with a big red heart necklace on a thin silver chain. "I do not have plans. Are you asking me out on a date?"

Chris turned red in the face, growing quiet and a tad embarrassed. "I guess I am. You're beautiful and I enjoy talking with you. I'd like to get to know you."

Sarah felt her entire body tingle, right down to her toes. That was one of the nicest compliments she'd ever received—and from such a handsome man. "Sounds good. I think that could work. Let me give you my number."

Chris put her number into his phone with the biggest grin any man could have. "I look forward to it."

Sarah walked back to the tent with her apron draped over

her shoulder to discover an even bigger line than before. Doug and April worked speedily, but looked over at Sarah when she approached.

"So, how did it go? Girl, we saw everything. That handsome man tracked you down like the CIA," Doug said.

Sarah stepped behind the makeshift counter and took the next coffee order, handing April a cup to fill. "Let's just say, we're going out tomorrow."

April handed the coffee to the customer then jumped up and down, holding hands with Doug while squealing. "Yay! This is so exciting. You have to tell us everything, and I mean *everything*, and we'd better be invited to the wedding."

Sarah smiled and rolled her eyes. "You guys. *Wedding?* Really?"

Doug put his hand on his hip and filled another coffee cup. "Oh, dead serious. That man is marriage material. I can sense it."

Sarah laughed, then took another coffee order, suddenly energized in a whole new way.

* * *

The film's wrap party was supposed to be held indoors, but due to the unseasonably warm temperature, it had been relocated outside on the beach. Starting around seven, it would probably go all night. It was the last hurrah before most of the cast and crew flew or drove back home. Even though everyone missed their loved ones, they had felt like one big family the entire shoot.

Katherine, Katie, and Erin feverishly ran around the B&B packing up Katherine's items, and the other celebrities staying at the Seahorse gathered their belongings as well. They all had flights back to California booked for the next day.

In the meantime, Margaret and Liz helped out where they

could, which included aiding Maria in packing up all of her cooking items. They would sure miss everyone after they left.

Katherine yelled from the bedroom, "Margaret and Liz, you know you're all invited to the wrap party tonight, correct? I expect to see you there."

Margaret stopped scrubbing the counter and Liz cocked her head.

"Did I just hear her say we are expected at the wrap party tonight?" Liz asked.

Maria laughed as she threw cookware into a bag. "Yep, and you'd better do as she says or you'll be hearing about it forever."

Katherine yelled again from the bedroom. "By the way, come grab what you're going to wear now before it's packed away. William is having his drivers take us all to the party. Be ready by seven thirty. I never arrive early."

The full-grown sisters ran up the stairs like teenagers trying to beat each other to the best garment available. They each ended up picking some beautiful tops, high-waisted skinny jeans, and boots.

That evening, William stood outside with his drivers and several cars, awaiting the group in the driveway. While everyone filed out of the Seahorse's door and into the cars, Liz nudged Margaret. "I wonder if Dave will be there …?"

Margaret sighed. "I doubt it. I don't think this is really his thing."

"Have you talked yet?"

Margaret shook her head and stared out at the window of the car. "No, we haven't had a moment to really sit and talk. It's just been small chitchat here and there."

Liz frowned at Margaret, then glanced discretely over at Katherine where they both winked at each other.

The setup for the beach wrap party was extravagant to say the least. The production really forked out a good bit of money to treat the cast and crew for all of their hard work. Elegant rustic tables were spread out along the sand with spring flowers, flickering candles, and gorgeous wood charcuterie boards full of different delectables. A large dance floor had been set up as well as a catering station with the finest food the area had to offer. Security cordoned off the entire perimeter of the party, mostly to ensure the celebrities that random passersby wouldn't be joining in. The lighthouse standing sentinel on the shore, along with the moon and stars, made for the most beautiful party backdrop.

The cast and production crew mingled, and when the construction crew walked into the party all together, laughing and joking, Margaret immediately took notice. Goose bumps dotted her arms while searching the bunch for Dave, but she didn't see him.

"Hey, Margaret. How's it going?"

Margaret turned to see Irene smiling wide and holding hands with Brad.

"Hey, Irene. Hey, Brad. So, good to see you two. I guess you're official now?"

Brad laughed. "You can say that. I finally got sick of the friend zone and made my move yesterday. Luckily, she felt the same about me."

Margaret smiled. "That's wonderful."

Irene grabbed a strawberry from the table. "Have you seen Dave yet?"

Margaret felt her heart skip a beat. "Dave? No. Is he here?"

"Yeah, well you know Dave. He saw the caterer struggling to set up the tents over there, and he's helping them. Why don't you go say hi to him?"

Margaret grabbed a glass of wine from the tray a passing server carried, ready to finally see Dave, and walked over toward the tents Irene had motioned to.

"Well, I staked it down pretty good. I don't think this tent is going anywhere," Dave said to the caterer as he brushed the sand off his pants.

Margaret tapped him on the shoulder.

Not knowing who did that, Dave turned around abruptly and immediately turned red when he saw who it was.

"Hey ... you." Dave wasn't sure whether to smile or not.

Margaret brushed some sand off his shirt. "I feel like there's been some distance between us, and I don't want that."

Dave's eyes softened and he gently took Margaret's hand.

Reflexively glancing over her shoulder in the direction of a noise, and Margaret saw Katherine's entire entourage as well as Maria and Liz pointing at them and smiling.

Dave winked at Liz before saying to Margaret, "Let's go for a walk. Head towards the lighthouse."

Margaret set her wine glass down and walked hand in hand with Dave towards the lighthouse. Arranged near the lighthouse was a whole array of fancy couches, pillows, and candles that were meant for the after-party.

As they got closer, Margaret could make out some people standing there. "Who's that?"

Dave smiled and didn't say anything.

Before she could ask again, Harper and Abby ran to Margaret holding flowers. Behind them, Bob and Judy stood smiling.

"Mom! Mom! This is so cool. Dave got us into the party," Abby said as she handed Margaret the flowers and a craft project they'd made.

"We thought we'd surprise you with our homecoming," her mother said. "But Dave had a better idea. So here we are."

Margaret ran over to hug her parents. "Oh my goodness! I could sit all night with you two talking about your trip. I missed both of you so much. We all did."

Bob pulled Margaret in for a hug and spoke quietly in her ear. "We'll have time for that. Read the craft project your daughters did, dear."

Margaret smiled and looked at the construction paper project that the girls had done decorated with pom-poms and pipe cleaners and markers. They'd drawn a little family. A man, a woman, and two little girls.

"Oh, this is beautiful. Is this Mommy and Daddy?" Margaret asked crouching on the sand.

Harper laughed. "No, that's Dave, you, and us."

Margaret felt her body tingle with warmth, thanked the girls, then stood up to look at Dave.

Dave immediately enveloped her in a tight hug right there in front of her family, and then leaned down for a romantic kiss. "I love you, Margaret."

Margaret held onto the hug for what felt like an eternity and kept her head nestled into his chest.

Meanwhile, Harper and Abby raced towards the ocean while Bob and Judy followed them, allowing Dave and Margaret a moment alone.

"Let's not let something get in between us again, OK?" Dave said while kissing the top of Margaret's head.

Margaret looked up at Dave. "There is one thing, though."

Dave looked up at the starry sky in anticipation. "What's that?"

Margaret smiled. "You should know that I love you too."

EPILOGUE

It was April and busy season was about to start in Cape May with summer fast approaching: The Seahorse Inn was booked. Their farm stand, The Cape May Garden, on Liz and Greg's property, would be opening again soon. Not to mention Greg's new restaurant, which had a planned summer opening.

Liz and Margaret went for a trail walk by the Cape May Lighthouse, soaking in all of nature's relaxing sounds around them. They stopped to walk down the boardwalk, looking out towards the wetlands and gazing at the osprey nests.

"This is so therapeutic. Life is about to get so hectic. I wish we could just take the summer off," Liz said as she watched swans glide by.

"You're telling me. I'm so burned-out from getting the B&B up and running and then hosting Katherine and company nonstop for two months. The place is doing really well now, why don't we hire more staff?"

Liz turned to Margaret. "You think we're ready? I don't want to go in the hole with the Seahorse."

Margaret smiled. "Oh, we're ready. I looked over our numbers the other day. We can definitely afford to hire more people. Why don't we take the summer off? We can pop in at the B&B weekly to make sure everything is running smoothly and work a couple shifts. I want to buy some beach cruisers and lead a bike tour around Cape May a couple days a week for our guests too."

Liz thought for a moment. "Why don't we come up with a plan to spend every day at the beach this summer? We can work our other jobs from the beach if we have to. I know it sounds crazy, but I think it will be good for us. Even if we can only manage a half hour at sunset after everyone has left, we'll find a way to have our toes in the sand every day."

Margaret furrowed her brow. "I don't know about *every day*. We do have kids with their own engagements, but close to it might work … kind of like old times. I think we need it after what felt like working ten jobs all at once."

Liz nodded her head in agreement.

"Did I mention, Donna, our old friend from high school, is back in town after her divorce?" Margaret asked.

Liz's eyes widened in disbelief. "Donna? You're kidding. What happened?"

Margaret shrugged. "She didn't get into details. I guess we'll get the full story on the beach this summer, as I'm sure she'll join us at some point."

Liz pulled Margaret in for a hug. "I love having a business with my sister. Now let's get home and get the ball rolling on hiring people to work at the Seahorse."

Margaret started walking the trail again with Liz following behind. "I'm thinking Dolly and Kim will be perfect in manager roles. I have a feeling it will all work out."

Back at her car in the parking lot, while dumping the sand from her shoes, Margaret's phone rang.

"Hello?" Margaret said, standing on one foot.

"Margaret, it's Dave. I'm calling you from my friend's phone because my battery died. I kind of did something today …."

"You did? What?"

"I bought a house on the beach in North Cape May."

Margaret dropped her shoe. "Wait—what? You bought a house?"

Dave's voice was full of excitement. "I know this may seem irresponsible, but my buddy was selling his rental house and offered it to me before he put it on the market. It needs a lot of work, but the price is right."

"Whoa. Really? Would you live there though?" Margaret asked.

Dave sighed. "Possibly. I'm not really sure exactly. I could just rent it out like my buddy did. I could flip it and sell it for more. Or I could live there part-time while renting it out part-time. It definitely will be an investment. You know I love a good project, and this one presented itself, and I couldn't say no."

Margaret laughed. "Wow, OK. Well, I have to say this is pretty surprising, but I'm thrilled for you. If you think it's the right move, then I trust your judgment."

"You should see the amazing sunsets that come through the windows of the house, Margaret. It's insane. It's near a neat little outdoor restaurant too. I met the neighbor, Chris today. He owns The Blue Heron Birding Boat by the bay. Cool guy."

"Hold up. You met Chris? The guy that runs the birding boat? He lives next door? I have yet to meet him."

Dave was confused. "How do you know Chris?"

"I guess I forgot to tell you. Sarah is dating him now."

* * *

Pick up **Book 4** in the Cape May Series, **Cape May Beach Days,** to follow Margaret, Liz, Greg, Dave, and some new characters as well as old familiar ones.

Follow me on Facebook at **https://www. facebook.com/ClaudiaVanceBooks**

ABOUT THE AUTHOR

Claudia Vance is a writer of women's fiction and clean romance. She writes feel good reads that take you to places you'd like to visit with characters you'd want to get to know.

She lives with her boyfriend and 2 cats in a charming small town in New Jersey, not too far from the beautiful beach town of Cape May. She worked behind the scenes on tv shows and film sets for many years, and she's an avid gardener and nature lover.

Made in the USA
Columbia, SC
03 October 2023